PEACHES I.

PEACHES IN SYRUP

JP JAMESON

© JP Jameson, 2017

Published by The Whippet Press

A CIP catalogue record for this book is available from the British Library.

ISBN 978-0-9955813-0-2 (Paperback)
ISBN 978-0-9955813-1-9 (Mobi)
ISBN 978-0-9955813-2-6 (Paperback)

Book layout and cover design by Clare Brayshaw

Cover image © Erikreis | Dreamstime.com – Work and pleasure photo

Prepared and printed by:

York Publishing Services Ltd
64 Hallfield Road
Layerthorpe
York YO31 7ZQ

Tel: 01904 431213

Website: www.yps-publishing.co.uk

Love many, trust few
Learn to paddle your own canoe

Sex is giving your body for pleasure
love is giving your heart, mind and soul

CHAPTER ONE

Sleep? Sleep is for wimps, not young randy executive reps. It's six in the morning, the central heating hasn't kicked-in yet and it's bloody freezing, and I don't care. Yesterday I got *the job*; the chance to see the world, the world of sports fashion. First class travel, fast cars, expense account, gorgeous girls; that's me, Jason Caine, Account Executive for The Doyle Group sports fashion. Milan, Paris, New York here I come!!!

Well it can't be that difficult, looking at some of the tossers who are doing it.

The immediate choice *is* more difficult, I could climb out from under the warm duvet and make a dash towards a hot shower in a cold bathroom, or go to sleep for a couple of hours until the place warms up.

Just as I thought, the bathroom is freezing and by the time I get out of the shower it's like a sauna with condensation running down the walls. How am I supposed to make myself look like the suave and sophisticated rep if I have to dry-off in a sauna and have a shave in a mirror that looks like bubble wrap?

If I'd gone to public school in the Outer Hebrides I'd probably be used to this sort of thing, breaking the ice on the loch and having a dip at six in the morning.

I did make it to the local grammar school, by the skin of my teeth, hated every minute of it and left at sixteen to get a job. Except the rugby of course, that was the only good thing about school, but that was only a couple of hours a week and a match on Saturdays.

In my last year we won the league and the sevens knockout, the first time the school had done the double. As things were winding down for half term the sports master took a few of the team for a lunchtime pint. We were to sneak into the tap room and he sent us a pint each through from the lounge.

Well one pint only just wets the sides, so we took a bottle each back to school in the inside pockets of our blazers and between lessons we were having a quick swig and showing off to the girls. Things got a bit rowdy and we were rumbled, sent to the headmaster and given six of the best for drinking in school.

The only other good thing about school; it's where I met my current girlfriend Sam. No we haven't been an item since sixteen, but I always fancied her, even then. We bumped into each other a few months ago in a club and started reminiscing about old times; it sort of progressed from there.

Sex on legs, all the lads used to drool about her, still do. Beautiful complexion with wavy brunette hair and a Caribbean tan. Quite tall, about 5ft 7in with all the curves in the right places. Always played 'hard to get' at school and told everyone she had a 26 year old rugby playing boyfriend who was extremely jealous, to keep the wolves at bay; well now she has. Anyway we're out for dinner tonight and hopefully 'afters'.

But now it's out of the sauna, back to the freezing bedroom and off to the first day of a new life.

"OK lad, next week you're on a sales course. Go with a positive attitude and don't fuck-up, in fact don't fuck anything, you're representing the company now." Stan, Sales Office Manager, calls a spade a spade and anyone who can't hold their drink a nancy.

He's probably early sixties and just batting out a few more years before retirement. Drinks like a fish, smokes like a chimney, a pipe smoker with red hot bits of ash that escape the pipe bowl and burn holes in the front of his shirt on top of his beer belly; it looks like a wok sized colander.

His one and only 'funny story' is about a couple on the night of their silver wedding; she stands in the bathroom doorway naked and says 'I stood here naked 25 years ago, what were you thinking then?' He replies 'I wanted to shag you senseless and suck your tits dry'. She says 'and what do you think now?' He says 'I think I've achieved it'.

"I've seen too many o' you youngsters before, wet behind the ears and blood pressure between your legs. Give you a company Ferrari and you think you can pull anything in a short skirt." Don't know where he got the idea about the short skirt, we can pull *anything!*

I've been working for the same company since leaving school at sixteen, mostly in the purchasing department processing paperwork and chasing suppliers to ship on time and transport companies to deliver on time.

The company manufactures and imports/exports sportswear; everything from swimwear to ski wear. Exclusive labels and high quality gear or the up-market 'individual' high street stores.

I made the jump from purchasing to marketing and ever since have been trying to make an impression on the Sales &

Marketing Director and his PA; what a stunner she is, and no I wouldn't need asking twice.

A dozen reps on the road plus sales managers, marketing managers, key account executives, directors, a chairman and the rest of the 20% who take 80% of the profit. See I've learned the 80/20 rule already! The sales and marketing director, Simon King thinks he's god, in fact, as far as I'm concerned he is. Spends most of his time having lunch and dinner, but having seen some of the 'models' he's wining and dining I wouldn't complain. No wonder he's on his third wife, sorry 'partner', after two very expensive divorces.

He seems like the sort of guy I think I'd like to be; tall, well built with wavy fair hair and a public school accent, early forties I would guess. Very good with the patter, both business wise and with the ladies; a bit Hugh Grant-ish with attitude I suppose.

Fire engine red was about as close as it gets to a Ferrari. A bright red two year old BMW 316 with 40,000 miles on the clock had been abandoned at the end of the car park by its previous occupant, my predecessor Terry; a bald fat slob of a guy who stank of whiskey and fags and bragged about his 'hit rate' with women on every business trip.

"Had a double bagger last week, that's two bags on her head in case one splits open. Great big fat lass, could slap her thighs and ride in on t' ripples. Had to chuck a bag of flour on her first to find a damp bit." He always wore the same suit with a shiny arse, ash down the front and dandruff on the shoulders, sweat stains in the armpits and a piss stain on the fly. God knows what his underwear was like, yet strange women were sleeping with him all the time, must be very bloody strange. I often wondered if he paid for it or just ended up with the runt of the litter.

I hope he didn't screw them in the back of the Ferrari, *my* Ferrari, oh shit!

Terry appeared from Stan's office looking completely pissed-off. Lost his license drink driving so the job went with it. Still wearing the same suit, stains and dandruff and probably the same underwear, and all of that had been sitting in my car seat for 40,000 miles, what a horrible thought.

I don't think anyone was too upset about Terry, they'd been looking for an excuse to get rid for some time. His appearance and attitude didn't really fit with the new regime of designer labels and a board of directors with Oxbridge accents.

That is since the take-over six months ago. Used to be a small family business until the old man died and his two sons decided to opt for a few million each and sail off into the sunset. Not that I should complain, the new group expansion is how I got the chance to become super-rep for the Doyle Group; well a division of it.

"And fucking look after it" snapped Stan as he lobbed the keys across the desk towards me. "Prang it and you're in a 2CV next".

Well all high flyers have to start somewhere, Richard Branson started with a mini van.

CHAPTER TWO

My first company car and my first week away on a training course. Buckinghamshire, has a nice upmarket ring to it like Middle Wallop and Upper Effingham. Won't go down well with the girlfriend though, we see each other most nights and she's quite possessive. Unusual for a girl, it's usually the man that's possessive, particularly with a stunner like Sam.

Got the shag of my life that night, spent two hours cleaning the Ferrari but it was worth it. It's amazing how much fag ash and dandruff you can get into a 3 series BM, should be in the Guinness book of records our Terry.

Took Sam for an Italian meal in the now pristine Ferrari, couple of aperitifs and a bottle of wine; you can't beat a drop of leg-opener for a good night out. Quite roomy in the back these junior BM's and the way the prop shaft just tickles your nuts as you move backwards and forwards. I eventually had a piece of sheepskin fitted to the tunnel; my mum never understood why it wasn't in the foot well for your feet, dad just grinned and said nothing as usual.

Sam, or Samantha as her mother insists, is very up market, at least by my standards, beautiful house, daddy has a Merc, mummy a Range Rover, little sister a pony and a real chip on her shoulder.

Anyway, after the Italian we drove a few miles into the country; er...'because it was a beautiful night and the stars were twinkling in the inky blue sky'. Honestly, I thought the view would be far better from the back seat, she agreed; obviously the bottle of Chateau de leg-opener was working.

It was quite dark in the back so I left the glove box open (BMW think of everything). Once my eyes were accustomed to the dark the glove box light was enough to see – well anything worth seeing! She was just wild. Wearing a tight fitting white top and leather mini skirt, her tongue was so far down my throat I couldn't breathe. She moved me into a corner, my head between the back of the seat and the door, my legs diagonally across to the other side. She straddled me and her skirt slipped even higher to reveal skimpy white pants.

Sitting above me she crossed her arms and slowly peeled off her top to reveal a low cut white lace bra, made to look all the better with a Caribbean tan next to the Persil white bra. Slowly her hands went behind her back and her bra shot loose blown away by the most beautiful pair of glands you've ever seen, certainly I'd ever seen. Beautiful pink nipples standing erect and as hard as grandma's sewing thimbles.

They weren't the only things erect either, she was sitting right on my lust weapon which felt like it was about to explode if it wasn't cut loose. She took off my shirt and undid my trousers, my weapon flew out like a jack-in-a-box to a great sigh of relief from me. It's not easy trying to keep your dick in cramped conditions when your brain is trying to pump a gallon of blood into it.

She moved her pants to one side and slowly forced the full shaft inside her, taking sharp intakes of breath every inch or so; well at least 8 or 9 intakes of breath!!!

She sat still, her hands behind her on my knees, her head tilted backward her wavy brunette hair brushing her shoulders and those ripe 36's with red hot thimbles standing erect in front of me. I raised my head and touched the end of my tongue on her nipple to an ecstatic cry of something between noo-ooh and noo-oow.

Love juice, or la jus d'amore as the French would say, was now running down the back of my dick as she started writhing up and down until we couldn't stand it any longer and with a cry that would have woken sleeping beauty she collapsed in a heap on top of me.

When I opened my eyes I could see she was still wearing her leather skirt and her nipples were like Ferrari wheel nuts. I slipped out from under her, unzipped her skirt and took her pants off to reveal a bikini waxed crop of beautiful curly brunette hair between gorgeous long slim suntanned legs. I eased them apart and put one on the back of each front seat. With one knee in each foot well and my balls stroking the sheepskin tunnel we went into orbit again.

We lay there for ages in silence until I realised the steamed-up windows were covered in snow.

It seemed like a great idea at the time, driving a few miles down a deserted country lane in winter and reversing into a field gateway so that, should the odd snowplough come past, we wouldn't be disturbed. I peered through the misted screen and it didn't seem too bad, maybe only an inch or two.

Getting dressed in the back of a 3 series is far more difficult than getting undressed, particularly when the various items of clothing are scattered everywhere and the only light is a one candle power glove box bulb.

I wound the window down and a cloud of snowflakes blasted in like opening the door of a mountain cabin in a Laurel & Hardy film.

Once the car warmed up and the screen cleared we roared off – well the wheels roared off but the car didn't move, at least not forwards, the back end slewed round and dumped itself in a ditch.

It's really amazing what goes through your mind at a time like this; the sack for trashing the company car on day one; has she been taking her pill regularly; where the hell am I going to get a tow truck at this time of night?

There was no choice but to leave the car and walk home, Sam's parents lived much closer than mine so it would have to be there, even so it was a couple of miles walk along a country lane covered in snow and in a howling blizzard, great end to the night.

It was well past midnight when we arrived and her dad was going upstairs as Sam stumbled through the front door, no bra, buttons open on her blouse and organ stop nipples poking through. Why does a cold wind have the same effect as a warm tongue on nipples?

I apologetically explained to her dad what had happened and how we'd been taking a short cut down the lane when the back end of the car slithered on the snow and ended up in a ditch. He wandered off to bed still with the fixed glare of his daughters nipples in his eyes. "The spare rooms made up. I'll speak to you two in the morning" he whispered from the top of the stairs in a whisper loud enough to wake the dead, and certainly loud enough to wake mother.

"I'm awake now", wailed the floor length pink fleece dressing gown topped with a tub of anti-wrinkle cream. Sue appeared at the top of the stairs her face reflecting the hall lights like a miner's helmet with a halogen bulb in it.

They say if you want to know what your girlfriend will look like in 30 years time look at her mother, not a pretty sight, or a pretty temperament. How can this change to that in one generation?

Suitably convinced that everything was fine and all would be explained tomorrow the meringue topped pink panther went back to bed.

I squelched along to the spare room when Sam pushed me in the direction of the bathroom, "hot shower first rep", she said as she peeled off her wet blouse.

I'd only been going out with her for few months and had spent most of that time trying to get *into* her knickers, having finally made it she wasn't going to let me out of them.

There's something quite raunchy about soaping each other in the shower and having sex standing up with hot water cascading all over you. Particularly when she insists on gently soaping your stem and bulbs first.

Absolutely knackered I gratefully fell into a warm soft bed in the spare room.

You must be joking!

Having cracked it at last and obviously not being Richard and the pink panther's flavour of the month we decided not to risk any further wrath by being caught in the same bed.

The following morning the snow had mostly gone and Richard towed the BM out of the ditch with the pink panther's Range Rover, no doubt while she was still chiselling the meringue off her face.

Don't want to sound prudish Jason lad, we've all been there, but probably not a good idea to be so obvious about it, at least until Sue gets to know you better. I know you're both over 21 but, well, enough said eh?

Not a bad chap Richard, took over his father's car dealerships when he retired to the Caribbean a few years ago. His father, Jack, made him learn everything the hard way by working in the repair shop, customer service, sales etc. until he considered 'Dick' was good enough to take over. Everyone knows him as Dick, or at least they did until he became group Managing Director, then Sue had everything with his name on it changed to Richard; better for the image you know.

We had the car out of the ditch in no time and Richard had a quick look underneath and gave it a clean bill of health. It also seemed that I had got away without having to face interrogation by the pink panther.

CHAPTER THREE

I arrived at the Buckinghamshire training centre on Sunday evening for a 9 O'clock start on Monday. Of the twenty or so on the course about two-thirds were women; nothing wrong with that, in fact it was bloody marvellous, I just hadn't expected it. All of us in out twenties. The girls weren't catwalk models but very attractive all the same.

Our lecherous lecturer Mark thought the same; he trains people from all industries so when a group like ours comes along he thinks it's his birthday. I guess he's forty-ish, very smart with a fake American twang, not your average lecturer, although wearing the ubiquitous tweed jacket and cord trousers.

We were split into groups of about 4 people to 'roll play' selling techniques. In my case it was me and three women. Two of the women in my group were married and one had just split from her boyfriend.

Now I know what you're thinking but sometimes life takes you by surprise, and this did. As a rugby player there's an understanding that your mates wives are off limits, as are happily married women. You just end up looking a complete prat and losing some of your mates who don't trust you any longer. But; single Sarah had been unceremoniously dumped by her ex-boyfriend Mike who, whilst on a mates stag weekend in Barcelona had met a hen party and fallen head-over-heels in lust with 'some tart from Essex', or at least that was Sarah's view, and that '...all men are shits with their brains in their bollocks'.

So, two married and one considering becoming a nun, better concentrate on the course and look forward to Sam at the weekend.

We were all staying at the local Hotel Grot, which obviously catered for those attending the courses and business came their way too easily. The food was inedible. Every guest in the place was on a training course of some kind, which all stared at 9.00, so breakfast at 8.30 was the order of the day. The bacon, eggs etc. were self service in chaffing dishes with night lights underneath and a steel lid on top, but they must have been there from the night before. The eggs were rock solid and the soggy bacon swimming in semi-congealed fat. So the healthy option continental breakfast it was, only it's February and bloody freezing outside.

In fact it's bloody freezing *inside*, must be another economy drive by Grot group management. Apparently there was a problem with the heating system and the Grot maintenance man was off sick. It would be attended to as soon as the local plumber could get here. I usually sleep in shorts but here it was full arctic gear with a bobble hat pulled over your face; but at least the shower was hot and the lecture rooms were stifling.

Stifling enough to make sure everyone was in shirt sleeves and open-neck blouses. Forget it, I'm happily in lust and the nun's not interested. Maybe our lecherous lecturer had turned up the heating.

As well as lectures and roll play during the day we were given team homework for the evening. A named item, its market price, Unique Selling Point etc. were given to two teams, one the buying team the other selling. The selling team had to come up with reasons why this item would be better for company X than the competition and the buying team had to decide whether to go for it and try to get the best price or counter with objections that the competitive product would be better. Each team had to prepare in the evening for the confrontation the following day. A confrontation that would be filmed and used in action replay to point out all the cock-ups. So we had to get our team prepared tonight for tomorrow's Oscars.

The Grot lounge bar had striped wallpaper with a random pattern of red wine, Guinness and ketchup. The carpet had so much beer and crap on it that the doorway to the bar looked like black ice and felt like walking on sticky tape. The staff wore the usual white shirt and black waistcoat with enough food down the front to show that they had been made to eat any breakfast we left, which is probably why they all looked pale and sickly, or maybe they had just cooked it that evening and put it on the night lights ready for tomorrow.

Anyway rather than sit in the cold plastic and vinyl Grot bar we adjourned to the local pub a few hundred yards away. A typical olde worlde pub with a buxom landlady, a log fire and a pint that didn't taste like Grot dishwater. Katie and I were to be the sales team with single Sarah as product support to chip in as necessary. Carol was the quiet studious type who took life very seriously and really would have preferred to have been at home with hubby making babies so she could pack the job in and be a full time wife and mother; everyone to their own.

Katie on the other hand was an absolute stunner, a few years older than me but groomed to perfection with elegant designer label suits, shoulder length blond hair and a wicked sense of humour. A lighter frame than Sam but with the same gorgeous long legs.

The other groups obviously had the same opinion about homework and the hotel Grot and soon all twenty of us were swilling down pints and having our buying/selling confrontations a day early. As reps do, the homework was forgotten and the drinking took over. The plan had been to have a couple of pints then a meal in the pub, the next thing we heard was the bell and 'last orders'.

Outside the icy wind cut through as we staggered the few hundred yards back to Grotsville when Katie suggested that we really should try and put a presentation together for 9 o'clock in the morning.

The grot bar staff had long since gone home, presumably bored out of their minds and the place felt like the ice hotel they build every year in Lapland. The night porter offered us a selection of miniatures and suggested we could drink them in our room because he turned the lights out at midnight; more economies from Grot group management. I wonder if they had ever been on a customer awareness course?

Having agreed that sex was out of the question we went to Katie's room to plot.

At some unearthly hour of the morning I woke up on the bed next to her, fully clothed and in a hot sweat, either the plumber was working nights or the heating system had kicked-in. The room was like a hot house and I was wearing trousers and a heavy woolly pully. Katie, on the other hand, must have woken earlier and was wearing a black vest and pants – and that was all – but she's married. Should I strip-off and stay or quietly leave, I decided on the latter.

The following morning she said nothing and we just got on with the sales course. It was a fantastic group of young energetic would-be reps, we argued the selling points for and against all day, taking the piss out of each other's performance and drank together all evening. Katie and I worked as a team for the rest of the week and neither of us mentioned that night.

As we checked out of the hotel and walked towards the cars I wanted to say something but it would probably have come out like corny crap so I said nothing.

As we reached her car she grabbed my arm and pulled me towards her, gave me the sweetest kiss on the lips and said "thank you for making the course successful, sleeping together would have screwed things up, but the course is over now" and she pushed a piece of paper with her mobile number into my hand.

After that I thought she was the most fantastic women I had ever met. From the first night on the course she wanted me, she knew I wanted her and given the slightest encouragement would have been there like a shot, but somehow she had ignored that and concentrated on work, and now she wants me for sure.

I went to see Sam as soon as I got home, it was like I'd been away months, she was all over me and couldn't wait to tell me she had been looking at apartments for us while I was away. I had been thinking of getting my own place for some time but hadn't planned on sharing with anyone, just a pad of my own to entertain 'friends' but Sam obviously had other ideas. It would certainly be better than the back seat of a car but was I ready to settle down???

CHAPTER FOUR

I went along with the idea and we viewed several apartments one of which was ideal and at the right price in the right location. Two bedrooms, one for me one for my junk, a small kitchen and a large living room with enough space for a dining area at one end and views over the rugby fields; staggering distance to the club house and the local pub.

I had to tell Sam that I was going to buy it, but for me not us; it was great to see her most evenings and weekends and she could stay whenever she wanted but I wasn't ready to settle down just yet.

I think Sam twigged something had changed, sex with her was great but I couldn't get Katie out of my mind. Maybe it's because she was a couple of years older than me, or was married and forbidden fruit, I didn't know, but I had to find out.

Having completed the course the next step was in-house training and even though I had worked for the company for some years I still had to go through the process, together with another new rep helping to expand the sales team. Lynda was to be our area manager and mentor, she had just been promoted and her 'patch' divided into two to make way for me and a new guy, Dan.

The first time I met him I didn't like him, he was such a smug, arrogant shit, very average in every way except for the way he kept his chin up and looked down his nose at you and with a constant smirk on his face as though he was superior because he'd been a rep for a couple of years selling bathroom products; probably toilet rolls!!!

Great Girl Linda, mid thirties, fair hair, slim, always wears blouses that are just a bit too tight to show off her beautiful boobs with the gap between buttons gaping open; just gone through a divorce (seems to be the norm in sales) and lost some of her sparkle. Apparently her ex was having to work late at the office quite often because the company was not performing, so one evening Linda had gone to his office wearing a raincoat, stockings and not much else, to try and cheer him up. Unfortunately his secretary had the same idea and got there first. They were just on the short strokes when Linda walked into the office.

Fortunately it hasn't turned her head, like Sarah on the sales course, but she now doesn't trust men and doesn't want a permanent relationship but still wants plenty of sex without commitment. Sounds like we'll get on just fine!

Although we knew each other from a distance, having worked for the company for some years, we never really met and Linda took it upon herself to get to know her new salesman better. There was a small exhibition pending in Southampton and Linda had been given the job of arranging the whole show and decided to take yours truly with her for the experience and to get to know each other.

It might seem crazy exhibiting swimwear in the middle of winter but that's when the retailers have to decide what their summer range will be. Gob-smacked doesn't really do it justice; we have the swimwear on display so buyers can touch and feel the quality, then we have models who will wear any garment the buyer is interested in so they can see how it fits on your average figure. The gob-smacking bit is that these models are constantly changing back stage but don't give a shit that I might be there getting an eyeful.

After a couple of days of this I had to tell Linda that I preferred to be out front and she would have to take care of the backroom arrangements because I didn't want to embarrass the models by being there when they were changing. She said models were professional and used to it. I said I was trying to be professional and definitely not used to it.

That evening we went out for dinner together, as we had done the previous nights. Over dinner she explained she was concerned that I couldn't handle all aspects of the job and maybe I should go back to administration rather than sales, and maybe she should have brought Dan rather than me. I said it was just 'first match' nerves and I would learn to handle it like the models had. I certainly wasn't going to have that prick Dan lording it over me. I know I've only just met him but because he's been a rep with another company for a couple of years he thinks he can lord it over me. He's quite slightly built and I suppose I could use my physical size and strength to put him straight but it's not really the right way to do it. He's a real cocky sod and will twist anything you say to make it sound bad, the sort of guy you just can't trust or turn your back on.

On the last day of the exhibition I handled everything with perfect professionalism, including naked twenty-odd year old models; maybe a cricket box would help to make it look less obvious. The exhibition had been a great success with orders from several premier accounts, Linda was over the moon and couldn't wait to ring Simon with the good news and, as I was ear-wigging their conversation, to tell him what a great job I had done supporting her and it looked like being a winning team the two of us (sorry Dan!!!)

We sat drinking champagne whilst the transport company packed and loaded the stock, "Mega meal tonight, Simon is well pleased with us – *yes,* I'm back!!" Obviously she was a happy bunny.

At dinner that night Linda looked a million dollars, full of confidence, success and wild party spirit, in a black cocktail dress with her hair loose in a slightly gypsy style.

As we were about to leave the restaurant there was a heated debate involving a customer and one of the chefs. Apparently the customer had been having dinner with colleagues and a client who was about to sign a major contract when this guy needed the loo but was boxed in at the back of the table. Absolutely desperate he took an empty carafe and filled it with steaming, sparkling piss. He was immediately despatched to the toilet and was about to pour the contents away when one of the kitchen staff appeared and said "What-a you do with-a de wine"

"It's piss" explained the rep .

"No ees OK, we drink in-a de kitchen" insisted the chef, at which point he gave him the carafe full of 'wine'.

Whilst they were being evicted from the restaurant everyone saw the funny side of it except the chef and the restaurant manager.

After dinner Linda just wanted to party and dance, which we did closer and closer until we were writhing about pressed against each other, "I'm gonna have you tonight" she whispered, "let's go". Having seen naked models all week and had Lynda all over me most of the evening I was gasping for it, but is it a good idea to sleep with your boss?

Walking back to the rooms I told her about Sam and reminded her how she must have felt when she caught her husband with his secretary. "OK Dan comes with me from now on" was the answer "you want to play second fiddle all your life, that's your decision.

We stopped outside her room and as she was trying to get the door open she dropped the key card. Bent on one knee picking up the card she grabbed my leg unzipped my trousers, grabbed a handful of hard-on and dragged me into her room dick first. "Take it or leave it rep"; well what would you do, I took it.

She took off her cocktail dress and opened the mini bar wearing black underwear and stockings. As we sat on the bed she said I looked tense and needed a massage. I stripped and stood there like a one-ended towel rail. She laid me on my back and took off her bra and pants revealing a clean shaved bush, or not-bush. She straddled me and slowly pushed me inside her. Unfortunately, with all the excitement of the last few days I didn't last very long.

Amazed by the not-bush I had to take a closed look and made up for being premature. It really didn't take long for her tension to be released.

The following morning we both had mega hangovers and I thought she was going to blame the booze and tell me she never wanted to see me again. Fortunately she remembered enough of last night to say she had a great time, we were a good team and nothing would be gained by anyone knowing about what happened. What happens on tour stays on tour.

CHAPTER FIVE

As time moved on sales were rocketing, Linda and I had a fantastic relationship and were unbeatable at breaking every sales target going. Linda was promoted to Sales & Marketing manager and I moved up to replace her as area manager but with a much bigger area and four staff including Dan who was really pissed off at being left behind.

With the new job came a choice of car; I was quite happy with the 3 series and rather than go for a bigger car with a small engine I opted to stay with the 3 series but go for the 325 sport with some real poke.

Dan was a real snide bastard who you wouldn't trust with your grandmother And somehow had found out about my relationship with Linda which was, to say the least, on and off; on when we were away together and off anywhere near home or office.

His trick was to drop very unsubtle hints that he knew something about the 'affair', initially it was in private when just the two of us were together but more and more he dropped these comments into the conversation when other people were there.

He had gone over my head and Linda's to complain to Simon that he was being ignored by us in favour of the others and that he never had the chance to prove himself.

Simon called Linda and me into his office to ask us to give him a chance at the next exhibition. He wanted Linda and Dan to do the next exhibition and didn't want a repeat performance of our relationship, which Dan had obviously told him about.

The exhibition was only 2 weeks away and I complained bitterly that I had already done all the groundwork and lined up some very influential customers and now Dan would get the credit. Simon then produced a list of customers that Dan had allegedly already invited to the show, *my* list from *my* computer database. That bastard had stolen my account files. Absolutely livid I insisted on going to the exhibition. Not only were Linda and me the best team in the company but as Dan's immediate superior I should be there.

Simon said it was overkill having three people at a small show but agreed as a 'one-off' providing it resulted in a better working relationship between the three of us and a purely business relationship between Linda and me.

"Hang on a minute Jase" said Simon as we were leaving his office "close the door". "I know you think the guy's an arse but try and get on. I've no problem with you and Linda as long as it doesn't affect work, I quite fancy her myself you jammy bugger". "Thanks Simon, I'll do my best but I'm not grovelling to that little shit".

We arrived at the hotel hosting the event the day before the exhibition opened to check everything on our stand was up to scratch and the clothes and models were in place. Everything checked out fine and that evening we all went for dinner together in the hotel restaurant with our two models. I must be getting used to this scenario but it was obvious the odious creep Dan was new to it as he spent all evening drooling over the girls. Linda decided to call it an early night and suggested the girls needed their beauty sleep. I suggested to Dan that we should try a few bars in town which I thought might give us chance to make up and him a chance to apologise for nicking my customer base.

Several pints later, with his mouth running riot, he decided to chat-up a couple of girls who were obviously with a group of young men about our age and who were not amused by his chat-up lines. "Why don't you come back to my hotel for the night" was not what these girls or their male friends wanted to hear. "Come on frosty drawers, let's have a look at your tits" was the final straw as two of the guys dragged Dan outside. Now, should I let them beat the shit out of him, sit back and enjoy it or do the decent thing and try to defuse the situation?

I'm really sorry guys, he's had far too much to drink and there's no credit in hitting a drunk, I don't really think the girls would think better of you for it". "Just fuck off then and take your arse-hole friend with you". As I said "OK, thanks guys" and turned to help Dan he swung a punch in my direction which missed the target and hit me on the shoulder. Totally pissed off with the tosser I planted one on his eye that a prop forward would be proud of and he went down like a sack of spuds and started puking in the gutter; to a round of applause from the other guys.

With him covered in vomit and regurgitated tomato skins we eventually got back to the hotel, I took him to his room, cleaned him up a bit and threw him on the bed to sleep it off.

The following morning I met Linda and the girls for breakfast at 08.00 but no sign of Dan. "Where the hell is he" said Linda "He had a few too many last night, let him sleep it off, we can cope" and so we went into the exhibition.

"What happened" said Linda

"He was pissed, got mouthy with a couple of girls and picked a fight with their fellas" I said, just as Dan appeared on the stand with the best shiner I've seen for some time.

"You bastard look what you've done" was his opening gambit, not sorry for last night and thanks for saving me from a real beating.

"Come here you arrogant pillock and I'll give you the other to match" I was fuming.

Linda went ballistic "you stupid buggers, the pair of you, calm down".

"OK, you were helping to build the stand yesterday and walked into the support rails, end of story, now let's get organised, the show's open".

I explained to Linda exactly what had happened but of course Dan claimed he couldn't remember insulting the girls and said I had hit him for being a little drunk. I guess Linda believed my version of events and the models just blanked the arsehole for the rest of the show. They refused to change with him in view so he was demoted to 'meet and greet' at the front of the display with yours truly entertaining the customers and signing the orders.

CHAPTER SIX

Simon was waiting in his doorway as we entered the office four days later, with Dan's eye turning a nicer shade of purple. "Jason, in here please". Full Sunday name rather than Jase mate was not a good sign. "I guess it's really not gonna work with you and Dan is it"

"No, the guy's an arrogant arse and always will be, he had it coming. I should have let the other two do the job for me but I wouldn't have had the satisfaction"

"Yeh, I know what you mean. Change of plan, I'm going to Milan next week and I'd like you to come with me. You've proved yourself working with Linda, now maybe it's time to move on. We've got a few hours travelling together getting there so I'll explain on the way. Are you and Sam free for dinner on Saturday, 8.00 my house, casual?"

"We are now, look forward to it"

"Don't say anything to anyone, Milan or dinner, OK?"

We arrived at Simon's just after eight; I'm never sure if it's courteous to be on time, a few minutes late or a lot late so we settled for a few minutes. Fortunately Simon lives not far from Sam's parents and as it was a clear night we decided to walk the twenty minutes or so from Sam's, and of course I could stay overnight at Sam's, best not get too pissed then!

Simon's house was quite an olde-worlde barn conversion on a generous plot with plenty of space between neighbours; floodlights in the garden to light the front elevation of the stonework and a crunchy gravel drive. Either Marketing Directors are paid an enormous amount of money or his previous two divorces were settled in his favour because this place must have cost a fortune.

Simon's gorgeous 'partner' Cheryl met us at the door, "well hello, it's good to meet you Jason having heard so much about you and your beautiful girlfriend Samantha, welcome come in". I only hope she'd heard about the good points of my successful sales record and nothing about my relationship with Lynda.

Cheryl is a tall slim blond with legs that go on forever and was wearing a low cut black mini dress and no bra with the most fantastic pair of glands pushing the dress out ahead.

The party of six for dinner included their next door neighbour (next door being half an acre away) Julian and friend Georgina 'George'. George and Cheryl were definitely out of the same mould. George was tall, slim but with jet black hair with an olive skin with the look of an Italian model; me and Sam, who could certainly hold her own in the model stakes.

I guess neither of the bimbo's could cook because the caterers were already there pouring champagne as we arrived. Perhaps I spoke too soon when I said bimbo, Cheryl was an ex-model (which is where she met Simon and the reason for his third divorce) who now ran a very successful modelling agency.

Julian is a senior partner with stockbrokers JPW and George is the owner of an interior design consultancy featured regularly in glossy magazines for the super rich and more recently with the sailing fraternity but more the ones with heli-pads than dinghies. Obviously your boss's partner is strictly off limits but George was Sophia Loren and Gina Lolabrigida rolled into one and I was sat next to her at dinner with her blouse only half buttoned and no bra.

The champagne was followed by an excellent burgundy, port and cognac, at which point the caterers disappeared and we were left to fend for ourselves. Simon who has travelled the world many times had a cocktail cabinet to die for with drinks I'd never heard of.

"OK Jules are you up for a session?"

"Absolutely everything, the full monty" came the reply "how about in the glasshouse in the tub" Massive conservatory with an equally massive hot tub.

"I just love this place, it's hotter than Barbados on a good day." As I turned to face George as she was speaking to us she ripped open her blouse and threw it on the floor to expose a magnificent pair of olive skin breasts with dark brown nipples. Her skirt followed the blouse to the floor and she was in the hot tub wearing only briefs, although that word is too big for what she was wearing. "Come on guys, more cocktails". Simon immediately unzipped Cheryl's little black number and another half naked gorgeous body was in the tub.

"Come on Sam, it's great in here, don't be shy we're all friends" said George in a reassuring voice. Sam was wearing a red silk tight fitting blouse with a black skirt, she peeled the top off to reveal a red lacy bra with a pair of nipples trying to burst out through the front door. Her skirt dropped to the floor and the red lacy pants revealed a hint of beautiful brown bush behind them, then she was in the tub with the other two.

I had such a hard on I could hardly walk straight, Simon and Jules were down to their shreddies like a shot but what the hell was I supposed to do. "Come on Jase, get your kit off" shouted Simon "yeh, just a minute" was the best I could offer. Cheryl then stepped out of the tub and came towards me, those beautiful tits sighing up and down as she walked. "Come on big boy, need a hand" she said and grabbed a handful of dick as she unzipped my trousers then held my arm as we walked to the tub. "fuckin hell Jase, you must have been at the front of the queue" quipped Simon as I stepped into the tub and hid my embarrassment under water.

"Now it seems to me, one of us has more clothes on than the others which is not quite fair" said Simon staring at Sam's rock hard nipples trying to burst through her bra. "Come on Sam, no need to be shy with us, it's no different than being on holiday on the beach" said George. "OK said Sam but that's as far as it goes. As she peeled off her bra I nearly shot my lot, only by humming tunes and thinking about rugby was I able to hold it back.

"We used to play strip poker after dinner parties" said Jules "but it took too long so now we just strip off, jump in and relax"

"We're not quite stripped off yet" said George and produced in her hand from under the water her black lace briefs, then stood up to reveal a clean shaven 'not bush'. Cheryl quickly followed with a cropped landing strip.

"That's it said Sam we're leaving", jumped out of the tub, grabbed her clothes putting them on as she ran and was out of the house and gone before I could think what to do. "Whoops said Cheryl, maybe we went too fast for her, should have stuck to strip poker for her first time with us. "I'd better go too" I said to Simon "it was all a bit of a surprise, see you on Monday".

I tried all weekend to contact Sam but she wouldn't take my calls or reply to texts or e-mails. I think I've really fucked-up now.

On Monday I went to see Simon and explained that his idea of a fun night had blown my relationship with Sam. "Fuck 'em, there's lot's more available out there. If you want to play with the big boys you'll have to learn to play big boy's games", which was not what I wanted to hear and I lost it completely. "So how many of the big boys in the board room know about your games?" I screamed. "That wanker out there has stolen my contacts and you've done fuck all about it, maybe it's time to advance my career, maybe it would be a good idea if I spent more time out of the office, I'd hate to say something out of turn by mistake to your fellow big boys in the board room" and stormed out of his office.

Simon and I avoided each other for a few days to let the dust settle, then I went back to apologise and hoped I still had a job. Simon also regretted what he'd said, having gone through three divorces he wasn't best placed to give advice.

There was no way I was going to back down on the things I'd said about Dan or the fact that I wanted out of the office and a promotion. "I've thought about that" said Simon "how do you fancy a move to a new position 'Marketing Development Manager?. You still report to me but we need someone to link between sales, marketing and purchasing. At the minute it's just three separate departments not working together. It means a fair bit of overseas travel visiting suppliers and trade shows, but I don't want Sam thinking it's me turning the knife".

"Forget Sam, it's over" I said. "When do I start"

"Just as soon as you hand your computer to Dan"

"He's already fucking got it, that's where all this started"

"OK calm down, start tomorrow, you can share an office with Linda, she won't mind 'cos you won't be in it much. Milan next Monday OK?"

"You bastard, this was already on the cards wasn't it?"

"Yes, but you had to apologise first. Nice body that girl of yours but if you really want her back you'll have to work at it, or take some time out and enjoy life a bit, she'll still be there when you're ready."

CHAPTER SEVEN

For some reason best known to Simon we flew with Air France to Paris and then on to Milan, business class of course. One of our stewardess's was wearing a different uniform to the others and as she delivered my G&T I said 'merci'. She took a couple of steps away then returned and whispered "I'm not French, I'm Italian, I'm on a staff exchange, I work for Alitalia" As she turned and walked away again I said "gracie", she turned and whispered again "You're welcome, are you going to Paris or do you go all the way"

"I'm planning on going all the way, is that OK?"

"That's perfect, I have a day off in Milan before I have to report back to Alitalia"

She walked away like a model down a catwalk; tall, slim, elegant with black hair in a pony tail and a beautiful tan; a figure hugging pencil skirt and gorgeous legs. Was she for real or was this an Italian wind-up?

"You've cracked it there you jammy sod" said Simon "Now start enjoying life" A few minutes later the stewardess returned, handed me a piece of paper and said" You were asking about a good hotel in Milan sir, that's the one I would recommend". There was the name of a hotel and a mobile number.

"Shit Simon what should I do?"

"Go for it you ass"

"But that leaves you on your own one night"

"Why do you think we came through Paris? You're gonna be on your own one night going home".

"But we don't stop in Paris"

"We will when we miss the connection; come on sharpen up"

"You'll learn, it's either sex or money that counts, if you get both you've won the jackpot. As Tina Turner said 'what's love got to do with it'."

As soon as we got to our hotel I rang the mobile number and arranged to meet for dinner down town near the Piazza del Duomo.

I've always found certain uniforms to be glamorous and quite sexy particularly airline stewardess's but as I sat with a Negroni on the hotel veranda I watched this stunning tall slim brunette walk towards me, it was unbelievable, and yes it was Monique (French mother, Italian father, multi-lingual and a body to die for). I really lost my appetite, for food anyway, my stomach was doing cartwheels just at the thought of what might be on for the night.

"I know a very good little restaurant a few minutes walk away, shall we?" she said. The restaurant was fantastic, quite small with vines growing over the ceiling and tables discretely placed to be very intimate. She kicked off her shoes and put her feet on top of mine as I held her hand across the table.

I really don't remember what I had to eat but I was thinking clearly enough not to slug the wine down and ruin the night. It seemed like we talked and talked about everything and nothing and then she said, "more coffee or a nightcap at the hotel"

"Yes let's wander back and have a nightcap" I said, trying not to be too eager.

As we strolled back I linked my arm through hers and she responded by putting her hand on top of mine. As we reached the hotel she walked straight to the lift and on to her room.

"There's Cognac and Whisky in the mini bar if you'd like one"

"Maybe later" I said "how's the view from your room" (must be the worst chat-up line ever).

"The view inside the room is much better" she said as her black cocktail dress dropped to the floor and she stood there absolutely naked, legs slightly apart, "let's have some fun".

I've heard stories about Italian girls who hold a knife to your back so you can't get off until they're ready. It wasn't quite that but she did keep those long legs and stilettos around me for quite a while. Athletic would be a mega understatement, she went on top, I went on top, back to front, front to back, sixty nine; on the bed, the floor, the desk and in the shower. I was more knackered than after eighty minutes of rugby, but it was fantastic!!! Absolutely Knackered I laid on my back with Monique next to me on her side caressing my stem and bulbs; what a wonderful way to fall asleep!

My mobile rang at 08.30, it was Simon, "come on you randy sod, time for work. I'll meet you in reception at the exhibition in an hour"

"Great", I replied, only I wasn't entirely sure where the exhibition was, other then Milan!!!

The phone call had woken Monique. I said I had to go to work but as it was her day-off she should go back to sleep and enjoy a lazy day. I slipped out of the bed and into the bathroom for a shower. Within minutes the shower door slid open and Monique joined me insisting on washing my stem & bulbs whilst I soaped her gorgeous tits.

We stepped out of the shower and began drying each other and kissing. I turned her round, with her back to me and put my arms around her whilst gently sliding into the golden triangle between the top of her legs. She lent forwards and with her hands on the shower door gave the most fantastic squeal as she reached an orgasm. I slipped inside and, even after last nights exploits, it didn't take long.

Of course I was late meeting Simon who just stood there with a big grin on his face, "lucky bastard" he said "come on, work to do."

We were looking for next season's range of skiwear; one piece suits had gone out of fashion, although practical because when you go arse over tit the snow can't get inside your jacket and down your trousers, they were history. Apparently more popular with men then women as they have to virtually undress to have a pee.

Two piece outfits in different colours was going to be next year's fashion. If possible we had to get the right gear at the right price and exclusive to us. There were the usual attractive models but this time in ski pants and bright sweaters thankfully, I don't think I could manage another hard-on for some time. Simon and I agreed to split-up, meet for lunch and compare notes. I found a small manufacturer on the outer edge of the hall with really good quality clothing very fetching colour contrasts. I was mid conversation with their Managing Director when a female voice said,

"Would you mind if I took over, Martin has a 12.00 appointment waiting for him"

I was about to say perhaps his 12.00 will wait when I turned and it was Katie from the sales course,

"Of course I don't mind".

"I didn't know you worked for Hamonds" I said "I thought you worked for House of Fashion"

"I did, it's majority owned by my husbands family and when we split I felt it was best to resign. I've known Martin for years and he's always said there's a job here if I need one, so there you have it".

"Just a job?" I asked

"Just a job; he's a nice guy with a lovely wife and old enough to be my father"

"Listen, I've got to meet my boss for lunch but I'd like to bring him back this afternoon to look at the range, say 3.00, and how about dinner tonight?"

"Just dinner?" she said with a wicked grin on her face.

"Just dinner," I said thinking I would be getting a call from Monique. "Sam's still the one then, is she?

"Unfortunately Sam and I split recently, so just dinner eh?"

"Sorry, see you at 3.00 and I'll try and sort something for tonight.

On the way to meet Simon I rang Monique, "Hi, how are you?"

"Fantastic" she said "what a great night"

"About tonight, I might have to take a supplier for dinner but I could see you afterwards"

"I'm on my way to Rome darling, I have a flight to Amsterdam in the morning, it's been great knowing you, maybe we'll meet again, Ciao"

Have I been used and dumped or just had the best night's sex ever with no strings???

We turned up at Katie's stand at 3.00 almost to a royal reception, Managing Director, Marketing Director and Katie, Sales Manager. I suppose the buying power of our company was considerable relative to the size of theirs.

Simon was impressed with the range and we agreed provisional terms subject to them being able to supply the quantities on demand and as usual payment terms. Although it wasn't quite 'in the bag' they insisted on getting the champagne out and taking us to dinner, ALL of us.

I made sure I sat next to Katie and whenever I could made little gestures towards her, she responded by putting her hand on my leg and giving it a gentle squeeze. As we left at the end of the evening we kissed formally on both cheeks and she said "come see me tomorrow" and gave me a business card with her mobile number.

The following morning I suggested to Simon that I would visit Hamonds and thank them for their hospitality and confirm that we would be in touch back in the UK. It seems strange that two UK companies have to go all the way to Milan to get a deal together.

Katie asked if she could see me that evening but Simon and I were due to fly to Paris that afternoon so we agreed to meet back in the UK.

As we drove to the airport Simon said, "We should get a good deal there, that Katie fancies you but you might have to give her one to get the right price" I said nothing but didn't like the tone; it felt like we were back to the hot tub the night I lost Sam.

We got into Charles de Gaulle late afternoon in time to catch the flight to Heathrow but Simon had other plans, dinner and the Crazy Horse 'with company'.

"Met this tart a few years ago, she's brilliant, I've asked her to bring a friend" said Simon

"Look I'm absolutely knackered, can I give it a miss?"

"Don't be wimp, life's there to be enjoyed"

We met these quite up-market girls for dinner, certainly a better class than I'd expected. As the wine and Cognac went down I began to feel better and in the party spirit. Simon suggested we should forget the club and go back to the hotel. We ended up in his suite with Champagne and Cognac. Having had a tough couple of days and being quite pissed the last thing on my mind was sex. As I made my excuses and left, one of the girls was busy drinking champagne from his naval while the other draped her tits over his head.

Was I in the right business, with the right company and the right people?

CHAPTER EIGHT

We got back to the office early afternoon, thank god it's Friday, a quiet night in and a lie in tomorrow. As I walked in to the office I shared with Linda she said, "well, well, what happened to you last night, you should have been back yesterday; don't tell me, Simon cocked up with the flight times and you missed the flight home". "Well the good news is that your apartment is clean and the fridge well stocked, the bad news is the decorators haven't finished mine so I'm still at yours".

Shit, I've only been away a few days and I'd forgotten Linda borrowed my apartment while hers was being decorated; and it 'would definitely be finished by the time I got back'; or maybe not. "Not to worry darling they should finish today and I'll be out of your hair over the weekend". Fortunately her car was at the office and mine was at home so a lift home was a consolation prize.

I walked through the door dropped my bag and sprawled on the settee. "Knackered darling, that's what trying to keep up with Simon does for you, I'll make you a stiff G&T then we can get showered and changed and out for dinner, my treat".

"Thanks Linda, but honestly I was planning a quiet night in, why don't you ring one of your girlfriends and take her to dinner".

"Alex will be here at 7.00 and the three of us are going out".

"Who's Alex?"

"She's gorgeous, you'll love Alex and I'm not taking no for an answer"

"Come on you've just got time for a shower before she arrives, a PTA won't do."

"What's a PTA?"

"It's an old saying of my mothers, if you don't have time for a shower always wash your Pussy, Tits and Armpits. Now move it!"

I opened the door to this stunning apparition called Alex, wearing a clingy red dress with no apparent visible signs of underwear and I suddenly felt that a night out with two extremely attractive girls was the best tonic I could have.

"You must be Alex"

"Yes, you must be Jase; very nice, I like a lot. I've heard a lot about you and that you're currently available"

"What's your poison? Available for what?"

"Bacardi & coke please; available as in unattached, no girl on your arm, or so a little bird told me".

"Wouldn't be a little bird called Linda would it".

Alex was like a breath of fresh air, or maybe a whirlwind. Medium build, wavy brunette hair, very fit looking with quite muscular calves and a really bubbly personality with a wicked sense of humour.

Linda appeared from the bedroom, the spare bedroom just in case you thought otherwise, wearing a similar dress to Alex but electric blue; I wondered what they had planned for dinner, should I take sunglasses.

"Oh Linda, you can't go out like that, get the scissors".

Within a flash Linda's dress was under her chin with Alex trimming her bush, which apparently was poking through the electric blue pelmet she was nearly wearing.

"It's OK Jase I'm a hairdresser, want yours doing?"

"Err – I'll think I'll pass, let's go"

A gorgeous woman on each arm and not a stitch of underwear between them. I could feel the blood pressure rising as we walked down the stairs. Linda took us to a fantastic Italian, all the time excusing her choice because I had just come back from Milan, but the meal was great, we just chatted and kept ordering more wine.

All the guys who came past our table stared at me green with envy, I was really enjoying myself. "Look, if you ladies want to go clubbing don't feel you have to hang around here but count me out tonight"

"Wouldn't hear of it" said Alex "let's have another bottle of wine and a slow walk home, if that's OK with you Linda"

It was a very slow stagger home but it gave us a thirst so we were straight into the vino collapso back at the apartment.

"You don't mind if Alex stays over tonight do you Jase"

"No not a problem but there's only two bedrooms so either you'll have to share or one of you will be on the couch 'cos I'm knackered and need a good nights sleep".

"Well we thought I would have that room and Alex would have the other and you can choose which ever room you fancy"

Oh shit!!!

I made a dash for my bedroom with two squealing nymphs after me and all three of us dived onto the bed in a heap. "OK as you're so knackered the least we can do is help you undress, just lie still it won't hurt"

They knelt on the bed, one each side of me and by the time they took my kit off I had the biggest stiffy imaginable. They both peeled off their dresses to reveal neatly trimmed bushes and gorgeous tits with pert nipples just ready for a good tongue lashing. "Spoilt for choice" said Linda "well I've already had you so Alex can go first"

"Both together" said Alex and with that Alex started kissing me, although it was more like mouth to mouth resuscitation, and put my hand between her legs. Lynda put my other hand between her legs as she slowly stroked her tongue around my fireman's helmet while I gave a stereophonic orgasm to both of them; just like stroking peaches in syrup. Who says men can't multi-task?

I woke up in the morning next to Alex, Linda must have settled for the spare bedroom. Maybe I was tired and pissed last night, better check, no, Alex was still stunningly beautiful. "Morning" she whispered, "sorry about last night, I'm not usually like that, must have been the wine, I don't want you thinking I'm a tart".

"I don't think that at all, it just happened and I'm glad it did, maybe we can have dinner again some time, just the two of us".

"Yes please" she said as she rolled over on top of me "but first I really would like you inside me, proper loving sex". How could I refuse!!!

"Got to go darling, busy day at the salon on Saturdays"

"How about dinner tonight, here, just the two of us, I'll cook?"

"Sounds good but I can't make it before 7.00"

"Great, come straight here, I'll cook something spectacular while you have a shower and change" Well something spectacular with pasta anyway. "See you later"

At which point I turned over and went back to sleep.

CHAPTER NINE

"Jase wake up, it's someone called Ryan, says it's urgent" said Linda shaking me 'till it felt like my head would fall off. In fact a new head would be a good idea, what were we drinking last night?

"Ryan, what's up?"

"Short of a man for the seconds, can you play? Didn't sound like Sam, whose the bird?"

"I haven't trained for ages, I've been away most training days; and I'll fill you in later"

"Don't worry you can play on the wing, be there 1.30, and I want all the filthy details."

Michael O'Leary, a great mate from the rugby club, nicknamed Ryan because of that other famous Michael O'Leary and his airline – got it? Much bigger than the real Michael O'Leary with broad shoulders and tousled hair; never really lost the student look from his university days. A bit scruffy and disorganised but with a heart of gold.

"Thanks Linda, err, are you going home today?"

"Are you kicking me out when I was the one who introduced you to Alex?"

"It's because of Alex I'm kicking you out, she's coming here for dinner tonight – just the two of us"

"Yeh, no problem, I'm going anyway, thanks for the loan of the flat, see you Monday"

I can't say it was the best game I've ever played, the faster I ran the more it felt like my head was going to explode, but we won convincingly, maybe they had bigger hangovers than we did.

It's not too bad playing for the second team, they want to win but also have some fun whereas the first team are deadly serious.

I normally play for the first team at number 13 but as I haven't trained for a while I've lost that spot so today I'm on the wing for the seconds with Ryan standing in at number 8 having missed three weeks due to injury.

Their left wing opposite me was small and fast so I had to nail him early and first time, if he got past me I'd no chance of catching him. Once we were a decent margin ahead they seemed to lose heart and we began to run away with the game. I was just beginning to take it easy when Ben, our number 13, screamed 'chase Jase' and kicked a high ball a full 40 yards towards the corner flag. Having wrong footed my opposite number I ran like hell and as the ball bounced over the line I dived at full stretch for a try only to have their full back flop all his weight into the middle of my back. I had wind coming out of every orifice and was seeing stars as I pulled out my gum shield and gasped for air. Nice try said Ben, you'll be back in the firsts next week.

"Guinness?" said Ryan as we walked through the clubroom door.

"Yeh, but I can't stay long, got things to do"

"Bollocks, Sam knows you better than that, now spill the beans."

With that I had to explain that Sam and I had split but I couldn't explain the details of why and that I had changed jobs within the company and that I had a new girl of two days ago who was just like Meg Ryan (Ryan's favourite actress, he must have watched all of her films several times)

"You jammy bastard, I thought Sam was fantastic, then you go one better, err, so is Sam unattached at the moment"

"Forget it Michael". He knows I'm serious when I use his real name.

"Well it's always the same, everything comes up roses for you. If I fell in a bucket of tits I'd come out sucking my thumb. OK, just give me £20 for the kitty"

"I've told you I'm not staying"

"Bollocks, flash the cash"

Several trays of drinks came back from the bar mostly Guinness and variations of Guinness;

Black & tan:- Guinness and bitter

Black velvet:- Guinness and cider (we tried champagne but decided it was an expensive waste of two good drinks).

This is followed by Guinness with a 'baby'; if you haven't had one before you should try it, but be warned!!! The 'baby' is a Guinness look-alike in a shot glass with Baileys floated on top of Tia Maria and drunk as a chaser.

The killer to end the evening is Black Death, Guinness with a large port poured into it.

"Ryan, it's six o'clock, shit, I'm off, see you all later" I disappeared to a rapturous chorus of 'swing low sweet chariot' complete with the appropriate hand actions.

How am I going to cook something special in 30 minutes? Fortunately, on the way home there's an 'OASES' shop … Open Always Sell Everything, Stupid. What motivates people to work all the hours god sends, do we live to work or work to live? Penne pasta, tubes are best, the sauce gets down the inside. Onions, garlic, smoked bacon, tin of chopped tomatoes, tube of puree, cheese and ciabata bread . Cracked it in 5 minutes flat.

Back home, hide the rugby holdall, get the pans ready, set the table, open the wine (always have plenty in stock), ding dong … "hi Alex you look gorgeous".

"Hi Jase, couldn't stop thinking about you all day, what's for diner?"

"Why don't you have a glass of wine, a shower and I'll surprise you". Might even surprise myself.

Alex came out of the bedroom with long wet brunette hair wearing my old rugby shirt (first team of course), which was actually 10 times bigger than the dress she wore last night, but she looked stunning; those long slim legs disappearing under the back and red hoops. "Won't be long, just waiting for the pasta"

"Well I'm wearing the shirt, you have to wear the shorts"

I went and changed into a pair of rugby shorts and a tee shirt. "Great legs" she purred, "never noticed last night".

After dinner we lazed on the settee watching the usual Saturday night crap on TV, I was running my fingers through her hair while she was stroking my leg, ever higher and higher until her hand strayed inside my shorts and her rugby shirt had ridden up leaving her naked from the waist down. So that was that, another early night and mad rampant sex, god what a life!!!

CHAPTER TEN

"Come on the sun's shinning, what are we going to do?"
"Oh I ache from rugby yesterday"
"Have you got any massage oil?"
"No just cooking oil"
"That'll do lay on your stomach"

She may be a brilliant hairdresser but she would have made a fantastic masseuse as well, as she sat straddling my thighs. The problem was the muscles in my back were relaxing but at the front the pressure was building!!! She slowly pushed her thumbs up the muscles each side of my spine from pelvis to neck, then out along my shoulders. As she reached for the top of my outstretched arms her nipples glanced against my back.

"OK you're done, it's my turn, I was on my feet working all day yesterday as well" We swapped positions and I began oiling her naked back sitting astride her beautiful bum. My hands did stray a little under her breasts and she lifted her body so I could feel her throbbing nipples. I put my toes inside her legs and gently pushed them apart then slid full length inside her to moans of "oh that's soooo nice". Gentle sex can sometimes be just as good as the mad rampant kind.

"Come on let's go for a lunchtime pint, some of the lads might be in, I'd like you to meet them" Just then the phone rang, it was Sam. "How are you" she asked "can I see you sometime soon, we need to talk?"

"Yes soon, I'm on my way to the club now"

"OK ring me soon"

"Everything OK, you seem startled" said Alex

"Just Ryan, sounds in a bad way"

When we got there Ryan *was* in a bad way, he looked like he was still there from yesterday, the Black Death had obviously worked its magic.

"Ryan meet Alex, if you can see that far"

"Hi Alex, nice to meet you; Jase you didn't take my phone yesterday did you?"

"No why?"

"I've lost it, don't know where I had it last"

"I'd like a word with you" said Alex

"That can't have been Ryan on the phone he's lost it, so who the hell was it and why are you lying to me?"

"It was an ex and I don't know why she's ringing me, I didn't want to spoil the time we're having together"

"Linda told me about Sam, you'd better decide if you want her or me and quickly. I'm going, ring me tomorrow, and I mean tomorrow"

"Alex don't leave … shit"

Oh well, no time like the present, I rang Sam and agreed to meet her that evening at my apartment. We agreed seven o'clock but the doorbell rang at six and it was Sam.

"Come in, I'm just having a bacon sandwich, would you like one?"

"No thanks"

"Drink?"

"Yes please, red wine" A glass of Rioja and a bacon sandwich, heaven.

The conversation skirted around the niceties of life then she threw her arms round me and said "Jason I love you and I want to be with you, I want us to be together, but as things were before you got stupid with that moron Simon" That moron Simon happens to be my boss and can make or break my career. Work versus love, you just can't be happy in both it seems.

We agreed to put everything on hold for a short time while I had chance to discuss my future and express my opinions with Simon but, as she said, "don't take too long I won't wait forever".

CHAPTER ELEVEN

In the office the following morning I ran over the events of the weekend with Linda who said she was in no position to give advice and anyway would side with Alex as they're old friends. She did however advise me not to discuss it with Simon as he thought he was God and his was the only way.

She gave me some history to Alex who obviously knew she was drop dead gorgeous, had lots of boyfriends but none lasted more than a year or so. However, Alex had phoned her yesterday and told her about the call from Sam and that she really liked me and wanted Sam to stay 'ex'.

The phone rang, it was Katie; could I arrange to visit Hamonds this week to iron out a few details for the contract, as soon as possible and tomorrow afternoon would be good. So I agreed to go tomorrow. Katie would book a hotel for me and I could stay over and they would take me to dinner.

Most of which turned out to be a load of crap. Katie met me at the station and as we drove through town she explained that life at Hamonds was becoming impossible. The Managing Director and Marketing Director were father and son, the father, Martin, being the company founder and all round nice guy, good to his staff and genuine with his customers. The son was an absolute shit, as is sometimes the case with second generation owners. He'd made it quite clear to Katie that the old man was backing off and he was taking control. If she wanted to progress she would have to take on the additional role of his personal assistant, very personal.

"The guy's married with two kids and is an arrogant arse, I wouldn't sleep with him if my life depended on it and certainly not for my job. Anything that doesn't go his way he goes running to daddy."

"Sounds like a real thrush."

"What's a thrush?"

"Sorry, it's a rugby club saying"

"Tell me"

"He's an irritating c_ _ t" Or an ALF, an 'annoying little fucker'; or to be kind ask if he's from Newark, it's an anagram of wanker. We both had a good laugh which put us at ease.

The car stopped in a side road in a very nice residential area. "Where's the hotel?" I asked "When's the meeting?"

"Actually it's full, honestly it's true but you can stay at my place and the meeting is tomorrow morning, sorry but I wanted to talk to you first".

The flat turned out to be one bedroom "OK so I'm on the couch"

"No; well, technically we've slept together before at Hotel Grot so if you don't mind we can share again, or you can have the couch"

Over dinner she explained that she was thinking of leaving Hamonds and setting up her own company importing similar lines but without the overheads of the big companies.

"So you want us to buy from you rather than Hamonds?"

"Sort of, I want 'us' to be you & me and you to convince

your boss to buy from us. Between us we have all the contacts we need, from manufacturers to suppliers to retailers".

Back at her flat Katie had obviously done her homework, all evening we talked about how and where to set-up, how much we would need from the bank and projections for three years. "Come on" she said "let's sleep on it partner" I'd forgotten about that!!!

"Look maybe I'd better sleep on the couch, I'm in a muddle at the minute with an ex who doesn't want to be ex and a current one who is happy with the present arrangement"

"Oh come to bed we've got a pokey meeting in the morning and you need a good nights sleep".

It all started very well, Katie in pants and a vest and me in my boxers and we were facing in opposite directions. Suddenly the light went on and she bounced out of bed, "It's not going to work this time, I'll sleep on the couch"

"Don't be daft, it's your bed"

"I knew you'd change your mind" she said, standing at the foot of the bed and peeling off the black vest "I've always regretted not shagging you at Hotel Grot"

Within seconds of her rock hard nipples poking out that was it, the blood pressure was up. She slipped her pants off and crawled up the bed with her legs straddling me. My weapon had found it's way out of the boxers and was standing to attention, "Ooh that's different she said" as she slipped herself on top and slowly moved up and down, her breasts gently heaving up and down to the same rhythm. It didn't take long for either of us to hit the jackpot together.

"That was just what I needed" I said "Out of the blue and absolutely fantastic"

"I told you we were compatible" she said "Now get some sleep, we've got a meeting in the morning".

Fortunately it was Mr Hamond senior and Katie, junior must have been too busy elsewhere; and she was right he was a very straight guy to deal with and up front about his company and his intentions. I asked if he intended to continue working for some years or had he thought of taking things a little easier, at which Katie looked decidedly uneasy. His reply was that, although he was in his early sixties he'd spent most of his life building the business and wasn't about to let anyone else have the reins just yet, even his son.

Were Katie's comments about junior the truth or a hook to get me to join her in a business venture and bed?

On the train on the way home the phone rang, it was Alex, "You promised to ring me yesterday, you bastard"

"Sorry I had to go to London"

"Doesn't your phone work in London?" she said sarcastically

"I'm sorry I stormed out at the club, can we start again?"

"You're breaking up, I'll ring you when I get back"

That evening I went for a pint with Ryan and told him the whole story, not that you get much sympathy from a six foot three No.8 built like a brick shit house who thinks I get all the dolly birds and he always gets what's left.

"If you take my advice you'll get away somewhere for a few days and sort out what you really want to do and if you give me all their phone numbers I'll stand-in while you're away"

Maybe he had something:- about getting away I mean, not giving him the phone numbers.

In the office the following day I covered the basics of the saga with Simon and asked for a few days off, starting right now. He was reassuringly concerned but I didn't expect what came next, "Is Australia far enough away? We're thinking of an Aussi brand of outback gear, you know Crocodile Dundee and all that shit, someone needs to go and have a look asap. Linda has the details, I can't go and she doesn't really want to, so ask her to make the arrangements and go".

Within a few hours it was done, I had a flight booked in two days on Singapore Airlines Business Class.

I kept my head down for a couple of days then sent a text from the airport to Sam, Alex and Katie explaining I was going away for a week or so, coward or what???

At Simon's suggestion I had an overnight stop in Singapore but ignoring his recommendation to visit one of his 'favourite' clubs I had an early night and pushed on to Sydney the following day.

I travelled on Friday to give me the weekend to get over jet lag and Linda had set up meetings for the following week with outback clothing suppliers.

It was the first time I'd travelled this distance through so many time zones and jet lag really catches you out, particularly if you've never experienced it before.

Saturday morning I felt fine and asked the hotel to arrange a rental car, it was hot and sunny so I went for a BMW convertible. The concierge had recommended a drive up the coast and into wine country, sounded perfect to me. After driving for a couple of hours the jet lag really caught me and I stopped for a sleep in the middle of nowhere, reclined seat, roof down, full sun. Yep I looked like a lobster!!!

Even when I woke up I didn't feel awake, almost like being drunk, you're looking at things but they're not registering in the old grey matter, and of course I hadn't taken any water.

Guessing where I was on the map there should be a small town a few miles away, and there was, a very small but pretty country village, and with a bar. I dragged myself into the bar and asked for a beer and a glass of water; well you can't just ask for water can you.

"Are you having lunch?" asked a beautiful blond voice.

"Er, yes I think I will" particularly if I could look at the beautiful blonde scenery. The next bit I really wasn't expecting.

"Can I sit on your dick?" the blond voice asked.

Now I've heard that Aussi girls are great and not backward at coming forward but this was unbelievable. Had Simon set me up? Hell, he doesn't know where I am; even I don't know where I am.

Fortunately there was an ex-pat sitting at the bar almost in tears with laughter, "should I translate?"

"I think you'd better" I spluttered.

"She said would you like to eat outside; can I sit you on the deck?" (just try saying it quickly with an Aussi accent) At which point all three of us burst into laughter as I tried to explain to her what I thought she had said without being too crude.

"Looking at yer face mate you'd better eat in" said the ex-pat who I later learned was called Mick from Liverpool; got fed up with being made redundant, health & safety and political correctness. Came over here for 6 months working in a vineyard and stayed.

The afternoon turned to evening and the cold 'tinnies' went down a treat. "Where yer heading?" asked Mick

"Back to Sydney"

"Not a good idea with a gut full of ale, jet lag and a face like a well smacked arse, anyway I have to go, it's your funeral. See yer sport."

"How about one for the road before you go, Mick?"

"No thanks mate, made that mistake many years ago when I was about your age. I was living with a gorgeous girl who said dinner would be ready at 7.00, don't get drinking with your mates; don't be late. My mates talked me into another and another and I rolled home about 8.00. She opened the door wearing her dressing gown. Christ, I said, I'm not that late. She opened the dressing gown to reveal a red basque and fishnet stockings. Look what you've just missed she said, and I've never been late since".

"We have rooms" said the blonde voice.

"Are you working tonight, or can I buy you dinner?" said the grilled head.

"I'm always working, my folks own the hotel, well I say hotel, it's a restaurant with six rooms, all available, take your pick."

"OK, only if you promise to have a drink with me after dinner."

"It's a deal, it's a quiet time of year; my folks are away on holiday."

I had no luggage, not even a change of clothes, just the shorts and summer shirt I was standing in. The beautiful blonde voice called Rebecca showed me to what she said was the best room and provided a toothbrush, comb and razor.

The room had the usual supplies of shampoo and shower gel, so chill out and enjoy.

"I'll be back in a minute" said Rebecca, and returned with a tube of after sun, beautiful and thoughtful too.

The restaurant was quite full that evening, but I suppose there's nowhere else to go, unless you fancy a 90 mile drive.

By ten o'clock the place was empty and the staff had gone home, as it dawned on me that none of them lived-in the place was empty except for Becky and me sitting at the bar drinking a very good Pinot Noir.

As the wine went down we gradually sat closer until our knees were interlocked and her hand was on top of mine on the bar. I started to tremble, like you do on those first dates when you're young, I was never sure if it was nerves or anticipation of what might be to come.

Becky had short blond hair and was wearing the usual waiters white blouse and black skirt with beautiful suntanned legs below.

"How's your face, does it hurt?"

"It's a bit crinkly like a dried leaf, maybe if you kissed it better" She leaned forward and gave me a long lingering kiss.

"You know what you thought I said when you arrived this afternoon" She said "Well, can I?"

"Please?"

"Come on, I've been working all night and you've been sitting in the car in the sun all day, time for a shower" and with that she peeled her blouse off at the bar, took my hand and led me to an outdoor shower next to the pool. "Don't be shy" she said "there's nobody around except us". I watched as she stripped slowly and professionally "used to be a lap dancer in Sydney to pay my way through college. Do you like it?"

By the time she was naked so was I, she grabbed my hand and we jumped into the pool together. It's difficult swimming with a hard on, it feels like you're dragging weed but she soon put things right on a sun bed next to the pool in the moonlight.

Now I'm sure she said her name was Rebecca but I'd misheard once today already, maybe she really said bed-wrecker! The colour of my face was quite pale compared with the colour of my dick by the time we'd finished, but what a night. I wonder if all Aussi girls are like this? The following morning I drove back to Sydney ready for the string of meetings, fashion shows and trips around clothing factories and warehouses.

Should we buy the 'genuine' gear or the lightweight fashion look-a-like? I asked for samples of both to be shipped back to the UK and hopped on my Singapore flight home.

I had a stop-over in Singapore again and went down to the famous Raffles for a Singapore Sling. The concierge had told me they always serve peanuts in the shell with drinks and the custom is to throw the empty shells on the floor. This I did but kept getting severe looks from an elderly English couple a few tables away who had the shells gathered in a neat pile in the middle of the table. It was almost as if they thought I was the archetypal English lager lout who dropped litter everywhere. As they left she turned to scowl at me one final time only to see the waiter swipe her neat pile of shells all over the floor.

I had plenty of time to think (and drink) on the flight, how to sort out my life at home.

All three or the girls were great lookers, in different ways and the sex was good, in different ways.

Sam was the quiet loving one, slightly prudish and definitely committed to one man with no worries of her ever straying. Sex was good but not fantastic and not much variety. Let's say she was a pipe and slippers girl who would be happy to be married with a couple of kids.

Alex was the wild one, happy to flaunt it and flirt with everyone, a real turn- on and probably the best sex I've ever had, but would it last more than a year and what's left when the sex dries up; or forget long term and just enjoy a bloody good year.

Katie was the business brains of the three, we could have long and meaningful discussions over dinner, then she'd cheat by sticking her toes in my crotch under the table or going to the ladies and returning without her bra and one too many buttons undone; but did she want me or a business partner?

The more I drank the more I fancied a bloody good year with Alex.

CHAPTER TWELVE

Back to blighty and back to face the music of three, probably irate, women who I'd had the audacity to text from the airport before I left to give me some breathing space and make a decision; which I had miserably failed to do.

I gave Simon a full debrief of the trip, including the outback suppliers and Raffles but didn't mention Rebecca. "So" said Simon "So what?" I said "So how about I buy you lunch and you tell me all about your sex life and why you desperately needed to disappear for a few days."

Lunch was long and boozy, as always with Simon, and I gave him Chapter and verse of my mixed up love life, including the offer from Miss X (Katie) to set up our own company. As usual with Simon things were black and white.

"You know the old saying: love many, trust few, learn to paddle your own canoe."

"Are you ready for kids, pipe and slippers?"

"No"

"Do you want to work for your father in law?"

"No"

"Do you want to set up your own business in this industry when the big boys can bury you at the click of their fingers?"

"Not sure"

"Could you live and work 24 hours a day with the same woman, no flirting, no away days, no time to yourself?"

"Probably not"

"Do you want 12 months of the best sex you've ever had with no commitment?"

"Sounds good"

"Do you want lots of travel working for me, see the world and shag as much of it as you can for a few years, then have a rethink?"

"Sounds good"

"Alex it is then"

"The problem is they know I'm home and I can't put off making a decision any longer, it's not fair to them."

"Why don't you come and stay at my place tonight, Cheryl's away for a few days and nobody knows you're there."

"I'd appreciate that, I'd also appreciate it if you'd think about my problem seriously and come up a answer that makes everybody happy."

"The impossible I can do, miracles I can't"

I went back to my office and Linda asked if I'd made a decision while I was away. I said I thought I had but didn't want to discuss it as Alex was her friend, but that in no way indicated that my decision wasn't in favour of Alex. She invited me back to her place for the night but I declined; if I ended up shagging her it would definitely rule out Alex, her best mate. Apart from which I had a mountain of paperwork to catch up with.

Friday evening is the usual Le Mans start with everyone away early for the weekend, or POET'S day, Piss Off Early Tomorrow's Saturday. I didn't want to go home and risk bumping into one of the girls or get to Simon's too early, so I got stuck into the paperwork.

Linda and me shared a secretary/pa called Sally who said she had nothing on that night and would stay and help for an hour or so. Quiet Sally lived with her parents and never mentioned boy friends, she had quite short brown hair and always dressed sensibly with what looked like M&S but she was a bloody good, reliable secretary.

She put together several options from the notes I'd made on the way home from Singapore. "Sally, this is wrong, that's not like you"

"Sorry Jase, I'll do it again"

She returned and stood at the side of my chair with a handful of papers. "I've done it wrong again" she said "Will you punish me?" As I looked up, her nipples were on fire and she was quivering "please punish me Jase". I slid my hands up her legs under her skirt and slowly pulled down her pants. I stood up and kissed her. "Just fuck me Jase, please" she said. I bent her over the desk, lifted her skirt and slid in from behind. Quiet, demure Sally went wild, thrashing about and swiping everything off the desk onto the floor. Afterwards she said she'd always wanted to do that in the office over the desk with me and she was available for similar anytime; then she left.

"Come in" said Simon "Throw your bag in the spare room, kick your shoes off and help yourself to a drink. The food is ordered, should be here any time."

"Pizza's or Chinese?"

"Wait and see, it's a surprise"

"Simon, what the fuck is going on?"

"Chill, relax and go with the flow"

The door bell rang and two very attractive ladies arrived and disappeared into the kitchen. "They bring the lot and cook everything fresh in your kitchen, you'll love it" I must admit Simon had one of the best wine cellars I've ever seen, quality and quantity, and it was going down like an angel dancing on your tongue. "Dinner is served" said a voice from the kitchen.

As we sat at the table these two gorgeous blonde girls served a fantastic meal dressed in black skirts and blouses, all pucker; and I thought it was going to be one of Simon's usual sex sessions. Duck liver pate, rib eye steak, selection of cheese all washed down with a New Zealand Pinot Noir.

Simon asked them to serve coffee in the conservatory and I had fallen for it, coffee was served wearing white cuffs a red bow tie and red stilettos – only!!! "Two for the price of one" said Simon "they cook and fuck, enjoy" So I did.

Saturday morning I drove home from Simons having made the decision that I had to sort things out with the girls and stop stringing them along.

I phoned Sam and explained that I had the opportunity to travel the world working for Simon and that it would get my name noticed in the industry and I would meet the 'right' people who could help my career. I wasn't ready to settle down just yet but maybe I would feel different at some point in the future and hopefully we could still be friends.

Hearing her sobbing at the end of the phone I felt a real coward for not meeting her face to face but I thought quick and to the point would be better than a long drawn-out wet hanky episode. As I put the phone down I had never felt so lonely and depressed in my life.

I wandered down to the rugby club and met Ryan who wasn't playing due to a badly bruised foot due to some great fat f'ing prop forward stamping on it last week.

"So how's your love life" asked Ryan "Well I plucked up the courage to put Sam on hold, but that's as far as I've got"

"One down, one to go then, but which one?"

"Come on, it's your round peg-leg"

We drank while watching the game, with the lads after the game and then at every pub on the way home from the game, so I'm not quite sure what time I got home or how I managed to walk at all.

On the way home we called at The Royal Oak to see Vince the landlord. He'd taken the pub a couple of years ago just before Christmas and wanted to do 'fine dining'. We'd called on our way back from the club with a few girls to introduce ourselves and he was really offensive to one of the girls just because her father was from Jamaica. We asked him to apologise but it only got worse so the girls dipped a tampon in ketchup and hung it on the Christmas tree. He went ballistic and threw us out but his wife Shelly said it was his own fault. Not that there was any love lost there.

At their last pub apparently he had been having an affair with one of the barmaids, Shelly had found out and sacked the girl. Then on Vince's night off she had asked one of her favourite customers to stay behind for a drink and had sex with him over the pool table whilst smiling at the CCTV camera. Vince only found out when he checked the film.

Sunday morning and I had just taken a bite of a greasy bacon sandwich, still in my dressing gown when the doorbell rang. "Alex, nithe to thee you, thorry, bacon thandwich, come in"

"You look like shit, out on the tiles with a woman or what?"

"Out on the tiles with Ryan; Guinness, Rioja and Jameson's, not all in the same glass."

"So you know we're meeting them for Sunday lunch then?"

"Meeting who?"

"Linda and Ryan"

"LINDA AND RYAN, when did that happen?"

"While you were in Oz; and while you were in Oz I've been celibate so you've got some catching up to do, starting now." With that she slipped her hand inside my dressing gown and dragged me into the bedroom.

We wandered very slowly round to Linda's where Ryan looked even worse than me. "You two had better have a pick-me-up while we cook" said Linda

"Why didn't you tell me about Linda yesterday you prick?"

"Forgot"

"How did you get her number?"

"She rang me and asked me out for a drink, nothing wrong with that is there?"

"How did she get your number?"

"You two share an office don't you?"

Oh; yes, so how's it going?"

"Great, just wants to be mates and have sex, no ties, fantastic"

After dinner we just sat around like two married couples, Alex and me were half laid on the settee, Linda was draped across an arm chair and Ryan sat on the floor with his back against the chair while Linda ran her fingers through his scruffy hair. As he sat there he reminded me of that other great No.8, Andy Ripley, big beefy guy, great company and a good friend.

CHAPTER THIRTEEN

Monday morning back to office grind and within an hour Simon called me into his office to ask me to go back to Singapore to meet an agent who was offering a supply of low cost unbranded gear. Is he psychic or had he been listening to the conversations between Katie and me?

That evening I rang Katie to tell her that Doyle group were looking at doing exactly what we were proposing. To my amazement she said she'd discussed it with Mr Hamond senior and he was prepared to back us financially in exchange for a stake in the company.

I quite admire Mr Hamond senior, or Martin, as we're now on first name terms. Tall slightly built guy, immaculately turned out, almost military style but no edge to him, he's done it the hard way and maybe he's happy to help someone else have a go, as opposed to his arrogant son.

I said to with Katie that it would be impossible to work and live together and see each other 24/7 and it probably wouldn't go down too well with Martin. She reluctantly agree but with the proviso that if we felt that it could work personally as well as business wise we would give it a try.

Off I went to Singapore wearing two hats, Doyle's and my own. The guy I was to meet was from a military family and had lived in Singapore most of his life. His father was

English and his mother a local from Singapore, he had been educated in England and his English was perfect; just as well because my Singaporean is pretty crap.

His name was Ken Reid, about my age and the business was really his fathers but he was a director looking to take over at some point in the future. Ken wasn't his actual name but it was as close an English translation as we could get.

He took me to a fantastic restaurant serving local delicacies like dove pate.

"Is this for real" I asked, "why not" said Ken "you English have thrush cream", with that I knew we were going to get on well.

Unlike junior at Hamonds he was interested in the business and in continuing the family tradition. We got on extremely well and I thought it best to be completely open and honest with him and give him my two options. Doyle had the reputation but would not sell under the Doyle name because of the lower quality and price. They also had staggering overheads so the range would not be 'low cost'.

Premier, on the other hand, was a new start-up with minimum overheads and would be very competitively priced so more likely to build volume and turnover. High volume and low margin was their business and he agreed to give us a 12 month contract subject to volume targets being met.

A few weeks later we had the deal agreed at both ends with Martin and Ken and, with some trepidation, I handed in my notice to Simon.

"What the fuck are you doing? Going off with this other tart to set up on your own with that decrepit wanker Hamond behind you, I'm offering you the chance to run a division of Doyle under our own brand you ungrateful little shit."

"It just feels right and......how do you know about my partner and Hamond?"

"Don't be fucking stupid I know everything, Linda works for me and only me."

"So you got her to shag me and when that stopped you got her to introduce me to Alex so she would report back to Linda who reports back to you?"

"OK, so what, it's business, I've pulled a lot of strings for you, I wanted you to be the next me"

"But I didn't tell Alex about Hamond, I only told Ryan because he's in the finance industry ......you bastard, you got Linda to shag Ryan just to make sure you'd covered every angle"

"Pillow talk, it's alive and kicking, works every time. You have a good future here. I'll keep this letter of resignation until Monday, think about it over the weekend; come in on Monday and apologise or piss off and don't come back … ever."

I told him he was a control freak and needed to see a shrink, walked out and went straight home, turned the mobile off and put the answerphone on; had a night in with my three best mates, Guinness, Rioja and Jameson's.

Saturday morning I felt like shit, my tongue was stuck to the roof of my mouth and my head was throbbing. It was as if I was in a dream, when I turned my head my eyes followed a few seconds later, like action replay.

A pint of ice cold water usually works but not today and I certainly couldn't face a bacon sandwich. The answerphone was red hot, 8 from Alex and 4 from Ryan, I went back to bed.

The doorbell woke me up about lunchtime, "Jason it's Alex please let me in, I want to explain." Against my better judgement I opened the door.

"Linda first asked me to meet you and if I liked you would I keep an eye on you for her because she wanted to help your career and could influence Simon on your behalf. It sounded a bit James Bond-ish and I thought it was exciting. Linda knows I never get really attached to a guy so I suppose she thought no one would get hurt; but this time I did get attached. When you went to Australia I was sick with worry that you might not come back or when you did you'd go back to Sam, I told her I thought I loved you but I don't really know what love is like, I've never been in love before, it's always been just fun and sex; all I know is I missed you and wanted you back. That's when Linda asked Ryan out. I guess she thought I wasn't reliable any longer. You look like shit, by the way."

"I feel shit and let down and there's nobody I can trust any more. I don't want any company so just go, I want to be on my own and feel shit for a bit longer."

She didn't say anything else just left, fighting back the tears.

I laid on the settee, channel hopping, drinking and generally feeling sorry for myself all day. Even Ryan couldn't dig me out of my depression; he called round to see if I was OK as I hadn't returned his calls. I opened the door to the supportive words of "Shit, why don't you slit your wrists and clear your eyes?"

They say if you give up smoking, drinking and sex you live longer; personally I think it's a load of bollocks – it just seems longer.

I greeted Sunday morning through another pink haze with the world in action replay again. The apartment was a mess with bottles everywhere and I looked like shit with two days growth of beard, but at least I'd made a decision. I went to the office and cleared my desk.

Ken was as good as his word and stuck with Premier for a 12 month trial period. Junior Hamond, Marcus was his real name, was an absolute bastard because his dad had backed us without asking his opinion. Simon started working on Marcus, wining and dining, a day at the races, he'll be in the hot tub with Linda next. Not that he's her type, a tall stick insect of a man with shoulders not much wider than his head, when he wears a jacket it looks as if the coat hanger's still in there. Skinny runt with a drawn face and veins on his temples that throb when he's angry.

At Premier we had a small office with three staff and things were going pretty well. Martin kept himself at arm's length but was there if we needed any help.

He had a yacht which he kept in Gosport marina and took me sailing on several weekends. Beautiful boat a 46ft Swann, I really got a kick out of getting the yacht to heel over; it's amazing how much fun you can have at 10mph.

He'd been sailing most of his life and suggested I was good enough to take a few lessons with a professional and get some sailing qualifications, which I did. I really warmed to him and could learn a lot in a professional way rather than the law according to Simon King.

Our first exhibition came round, quite a small one in a city hotel so a good place to start. The only models we knew worked for Cheryl and guess what, they were all unavailable for the dates we needed. "Sod it" said Katie "we'll do it ourselves"

"We who?"

"Are you up for it Vikki" asked Katie .

"Yeah great, let's do it."

Our receptionist, PA and girl Friday, Vikki, had a real bubbly personality and quite a fit body as well. "So, Vikki and who?"

"Me" said Katie.

Well why not, it keeps the cost down and they can hold their own against any model. The show was a success and everybody was on a high when it closed. "OK Vikki, thanks for your help, get out of here and we'll see you and the others at the restaurant at 8.00"

I went into the dressing room to help pack the stock and Katie was standing in front of the mirror in a black bra and pants. She looked at me in the mirror and didn't move. I took my shirt off, dropped my trousers, walked up behind her, brushed her hair to one side and kissed her neck. She put her hands behind her and slid her fingers inside my shorts, I slid my fingers inside the front of her pants. Further and further down until I reached the soft moist centre of the orgasmic universe. Very slowly I stroked my fingers around until she gasped and shuddered as if the whole orgasm had gone right through her body.

Her legs crumpled and I laid her on the pile of soft clothes. As I opened her legs and slowly slid inside her she opened her eyes and whispered "I love you, don't ever stop fucking me"

As we laid there afterwards I couldn't help ask one question. "You've started shaving"

"All the models do, it saves any embarrassing incidents that look like you have a hedgehog in your pants and if you like it I'll keep it shaved. Now come on we're late for dinner."

The following morning I rang Martin to tell him the good news and to tell him that Katie and me were a couple and going to move in together. "Come down to Gosport on Sunday, both of you, we'll take the yacht out for a couple of hours and then I'll buy you lunch, it's going to be a sunny day but cold, so wrap up."

Martin's yacht was a 46ft Swan with a dark blue hull and white sails. It would sleep six comfortably in 3 cabins with another two in the saloon if pushed. He quite often went to France or Spain with a couple of mates for a few days away and bring back a cabin full of wine. It was great sailing weather, sunny but with a 20 knot cool breeze from the North West which was perfect for a run out to the Needles.

We had a great sail but heading back up the Solent Martin suddenly went very quiet and said he didn't feel well, his arms ached and his lips were going blue. Katie took the wheel while I radioed for an ambulance to be waiting when we got back, which would be about 15 minutes. Martin passed out and I laid him on the deck with his head sideways and his feet raised, it looked like a heart attack but I'm no doctor.

The paramedics arrived just as we did and as they leaned over him one of them looked up at me and shook his head.

I don't know if I felt more sorry for Martin or myself, having lost a mentor and a financier.

What happens now, Mrs Hamond died a few years ago and Marcus would get the lot. The solicitor explained that that was not quite the case; Martin has arranged things such that if anything should happen to him whilst Premier was still worthless his share would revert to the company. If it had any value Katie and me would have the option to buy them at market value. It was worthless but with a fair amount of debt owed to Hamond, or Marcus.

I tried to arrange a meeting with Marcus but he was having none of it. Not only did he refuse to meet me, he lodged an official complaint that Katie and me had murdered his father to gain control of the company whilst it was still of little value but growing at a considerable pace.

We were questioned independently by the police, the yacht was impounded and Marcus and Simon had a field day with the media. Nobody wanted to be associated with Premier.

The post mortem and the coroners report concluded that Martin died of a heart attack and there was no foul play. Unfortunately it was all too late for Premier.

My phone had been red hot with literally hundreds of calls, from the media, friends saying it would all be OK and arseholes wanting to bring back hanging for mercenary murderers like me.

I walked into town and bought a new SIM card and phone number and cut the old one into a million pieces and put one piece in every waste bin in Gosport.

I wandered down to the marina to have one last look at the yacht and bumped into Tom Clifford, the man who had helped me with professional sailing training and through exams to Coastal skipper. Tom had sailed all his life from his days in the navy to delivering yachts to customers and training them how to get the best out of them. He even had his own boat yard when he was younger; now semi retired but can't stop sailing and helping others to learn.

"Sorry to hear about Martin and the aftermath with you and Marcus."

"Thanks Tom, it's all over now, the company's gone, Katie couldn't stand the strain and we split up, so she's gone as well."

"Why don't you disappear for a couple of months 'till things die down?"

"Like where?"

"The high seas. A round the world yacht race left in October, I did the training for those with no sailing experience. Come up to the office, I'll show you."

The only previous long distance sailing I'd done was a complete cock-up. Tom Clifford and three crew were commissioned to deliver a 70 foot ocean racing yacht from Falmouth to Lagos in the Algarve, Portugal. The yacht had just completed a full refit costing several hundred thousand pounds and was now fitted with the latest sat-nav equipment and all mod cons above and below deck.

With a good weather forecast we left Falmouth one bright clear morning heading for the coast of Brest and the Bay of Biscay. We had a calm, clear night crossing the English Channel with a steady Westerly breeze. With four of us on board all with at least some sailing experience and Tom with a lifetimes we decided on two watches of four hours each. I was on watch with Tom while Jerry and Hans took the other, well we couldn't have Tom and Jerry together, could we?

Jerry was an old friend of Tom's and had been pleasure sailing most of his life and at the ripe old age of 60 had taken retirement from the Civil service to spend more time sailing. I'd met Jerry before but not Hans who was probably early fifties and came across as the archetypal German, first there with the towel on the sunbed, very precise and formal; very good at barking orders but not so good at taking them.

No longer had we left Brest to port than the sky began to cloud over and the breeze stiffened. Within a couple of hours the rain started and the wind picked up to 20 knots.

The options were to stick to our course and head directly for La Corunna or follow the French coast and then west along the northern coast of Spain. We sailed our planned course for a few hours and the weather held steady so we decided to stick with plan A.

At just about the point of no return the weather turned stormy and the sea whipped-up. The yacht was an ocean racer so we may be uncomfortable for a while but should be safe enough.

At the end of my watch as I crawled into my bunk next to the mast it suddenly felt like a glass of cold water was being thrown into my face. I put a torch light down the gap between the cabin floor and the mast and the bilge was full of water. I turned the bilge pumps on and dragged Tom from his bunk. The bilge pumps weren't working and the yacht was taking water. On closer inspection it was running rain water through the deck and sea water crashing onto the deck and through the hatch seals.

With Jerry on the helm we put Hans on the manual bilge pump, much to his displeasure, as he pointed out he was a 'technician' not a labourer.

We lifted the cabin floor until we found the bilge pumps and checked that the wires were connected correctly – they were, albeit under two feet of salt and rain water. I traced the wiring back to the navigation station and all seemed intact until I removed the control panel and found the bilge pumps were not connected. What an idiot, why didn't I start at the dry end of the wires, as Hans Deutsch Technic was quick to point out. You may gather that international relations were not improving so I told Hans to keep pumping for a couple of hours just to make sure.

The storm worsened and the water continued pouring in with the bilge pumps just about coping.

On night watch it's better for night vision to have all white lights off but the nav station has a red light above it for night navigation which doesn't really affect the helmsman's night vision – except Hans!!! At watch change, if Hans took the helm and I went below and turned the nav light on he would bellow 'turn that fucking light off', so I left it on a bit longer.

At the next watch change I took the helm and Hans said 'now I show you how to do this correctly'. As he disappeared into the darkness below there was an almighty crash; Hans had gone arse-over-tit into the galley and taken Jerry out with him. As it turned out Jerry had a broken rib and Hans a sprained ankle – great! With Jerry and Hans out of action Tom and I decided on two hour watches alternating him and me so we dropped the sails and motored at 5 knots.

The next night with Jerry, Hans and Tom tucked in their bunks I was flitting between the deck and the sat nav with the yacht on auto pilot watching the world go by on the computer screen and every few minutes poking my head above deck to check the sea around us. We were not far off the north coast of Spain and La Corunna when I saw a westerly marker off the starboard bow. The marker was the west tip of Spain and we were heading the wrong side of it towards the rocks. The sat-nav showed us on course and to the west of any land; if in doubt play safe and trust your instinct.

I took the helm in the raging storm and turned the yacht westerly out to sea. The change of direction woke Tom and he agreed it was the right decision. With only two able-bodied sailors looking and feeling like we'd spend several days in a washing machine we decided to put into La Corunna. Sod's law, by the time we had negotiated a berth and tied up the storm had passed. The sat-nav showed us 3km inland in a car park; it obviously hadn't been set up correctly.

It was early evening and ashore the neon lights of Hotel Oceanica had just lit up. 'That's me, I'm off to the hotel, see you later'.

As I walked up the shiny, black marble steps of the hotel, past the doorman and towards reception I slowly realised that I hadn't had a wash, shave or change of clothes for several days. Sod it; I went to reception and asked for a room for a few nights. This very pretty, young Spanish lady looked me slowly up and down and said si!

I had a long, hot shower using most of the toiletries provided by the hotel, a shave and changed into clean clothes dowsed in after shave to hide the smell of sea water. I went back to reception and apologised to the receptionist, Anna, and offered to buy her a drink when she finished work at 8.00 and explain why I had looked such a mess.

I went back to the yacht for the rest of my gear and told Tom I was going no further in that yacht. "I agree" he said "How about dinner"

"Already spoken for" I replied

"Fuck me! We've only been here a couple of hours and you've pulled already?"

When I got back to the hotel Anna had moved my things from the 'cupboard' she had put me in to a large harbour view room and sent my 'horeeble clothes' to the laundry. As a thank you I took her to a restaurant of her choice which served fantastic tapas and local red wine. I asked her back for a night-cap but she said it was against hotel rules so why not have a night-cap at her place only a ten minute stroll away.

I could tell you how fantastic it was but after several days with only a few hours sleep I can't remember, but breakfast in bed with a small, slim, black haired, thick black bush Spanish beauty was something I will never forget.

CHAPTER FOURTEEN

Back in England I took Tom's advice and agreed to join the round the world yacht race. Eight 65 foot yachts set off from Gosport in October with three professional crew on each yacht, a skipper and two watch leaders, the rest having some or no sailing experience.

The race is divide into seven 'legs' and a birth can be bought for one or more legs or the whole circumnavigation, with a maximum crew of thirteen working a two watch system, five on watch, five sleeping plus the skipper and 'mother watch' one from each watch work together for 24 hours cooking and cleaning. Don't knock it, at least between dinner and breakfast they get a full nights sleep, unlike the others who are up and down every 4 hours.

"The race left England in October and spent Christmas and New Year in St. Lucia in the Caribbean. Next stop Panama, then through the canal to Tahiti, if you get your skates on you can meet them there. There are a few berths left and I can contact one of the skippers and vouch for you."

"I'm not exactly flush at the minute, you know."

"Do one leg and see how it goes, Tahiti to Tonga to Auckland to Sydney. Sydney is a major stop over for 14 days to get the yachts out of the water and have their bottoms scrubbed. Sell the car and go, make the next decision in Sydney."

Tom knew my life history as we'd become good friends during the sailing courses I'd done with him. I gave him my new phone number and asked him to tell Ryan what I was doing but nobody else.

I caught an Air New Zealand flight, with a change in Los Angeles, which then went on to Auckland via Tahiti. Why don't Americans understand 'in transit?' Why do you have to queue for hours to get in and hours to get out when all you wanted to do was pass through and change planes?

I remember going to the Caribbean through Puerto Rico and the immigration officer asking 'business or pleasure?' I said neither really I'm just passing through. He said it has to be one or the other they're the only options on the form. I said OK pleasure but it hasn't been, standing in line for hours when all I want to do is get a plane out of here.

Fortunately LAX has a transit lounge, looks more like a refugee camp but at least it avoids the queuing. Even better the first flight was late and, as a large number of the passengers were going on to Auckland, the NZ flight waited for us. We were whistled through the lounge and onto the next flight in minutes. Now America, *that's* 'in transit'.

Having spent 10 hours getting to LA I had another several Bombay Saphire hours to while away on the flight to Tahiti.

I arrived at the hotel in Papietee a few days before the yachts were due in, to get over the jet lag and catch some sun as there's no shelter on the deck of an ocean racing yacht.

The hotel was very grand, the rooms were woven straw huts built on stilts over the lagoon; about 800 yards out was a reef which calmed the Pacific to a mill pond inside the lagoon. The centre piece of the sitting area was a glass floor to watch the fish swimming below.

I decided to have dinner in the hotel that night but found it was all twosomes, honeymooners and anniversaries; people who'd flown half way round the world to be together when they already lived together. I tried to strike up a conversation with the bar maid but other than her name was Kim she wasn't interested, so I had dinner and an early night.

The following morning I wandered down to the main dock to see if any of the yachts had arrived but no sign.

Next to the main dock is a massive cruise ship dock which would probably carry ten times more people than live in Papietee, fortunately it was empty today. Next to the dock is the high street, across from which is a line of restaurants and bars and one street back is the market, selling mostly fish and fruit. I seemed drawn back to the high street, well it's never too early to sample the local brew is it?

I meandered up and down the line of restaurants and bars and even found one that offered 'English style fish & chips', so I gave that a miss. I've never understood why people go to the Costa Del whatever and search out The Red Lion, drink English beer, eat fish and chips and watch English football on TV. Why not stay at home and rent a sun bed, it's much cheaper.

I found a great little place which served a kind of local fish tapas which I thought I would try tonight. It's difficult to understand the local dialect but the language is basically French so if you were any good at school you'll probably pick up some of the conversation; anyway most waiters speak enough English so you don't need to bother.

I had a lazy afternoon on the beach then tried the hotel bar again, this time it was a waiter who was very polite but wasn't going to get into a conversation with the guests. The loving couples were all there again. If it was anything like last night the place would be deserted by nine o'clock. They'd all gone back to their huts to have a risque bonk on the glass floor and hoped that Davy Jones wasn't getting an eyeful.

I went down town and had the tapas I had promised myself at lunchtime. I called in a bar on the way back and found Kim serving drinks; on her night off she works at her mates bar. She couldn't apologise enough for not chatting at the hotel but the rules don't allow it, be polite but don't be familiar.

Tomorrow was her day off so I asked if she would show me round the island; she would but no car and as I hadn't pre-booked a rental it was unlikely I would get one at short notice.

I explained that I was in Tahiti waiting for a round the world yacht race to arrive when she announced that she had a boat and as I liked boats we could sail around the sheltered side of the island. When I say boat it was like a big canoe with a stabilizer and a sail, but what the hell it's something to do.

I ordered a picnic and beers in a cool box from the hotel and met her at the locals dock the following morning. She looked completely different, out of the starchy hotel uniform and in a tee shirt and shorts, not very tall and slightly built with long jet black hair. We sailed for about an hour then beached the boat and stopped for a beer and a swim.

I honestly had no intention of doing anything when she suddenly popped up from under the water, put her arms around me and gave me a kiss. One thing led to another and before long we were naked on the beach. She had a gorgeous body, small breasts with rock hard nipples and a jet black bush to match her hair. She certainly knew what she was doing and insisted on going on top, who am I to complain?

We swam naked in the sea and then sailed back to Papietee. When I saw her in the hotel it was the usual polite service as always, but with a certain smile on her face.

CHAPTER FIFTEEN

The following morning I wandered down to the main dock and two of the yachts had arrived with another two on the horizon only a few miles behind. I introduced myself to Jim, the skipper of the second yacht that had just tied-up.

"Ah, right first time, Tom called and said you would be joining us, we've got two leaving us here so you're on Diana with us." We've got three spare bunks so pick whichever you want but if you take my advice you'll stay in the hotel until the day before we leave, it's hot, steamy and a bit smelly down there in the bear pit."

I decided to save money and rough it with the rest of the crew and moved on board the following day.

He was right about the bear pit it was like a Chinese laundry, hot and steamy with damp, salty clothes draped everywhere. The yachts have 'water makers' on board that purify sea water but if all the storage tanks are full the yacht is heavy and relatively slow so we only make enough fresh water to drink, cook and the occasional shower. The laundry is done on the floor as you shower or in the rain and sea spray as you wear it. Sea water mid ocean is much less salty than near the beach so it's not too bad, still a little bit salty/sticky and it never seems to dry fully.

The yachts were 65ft Bruce Farr open back ocean racers built for speed but capable of crashing through heavy weather. Down below, the bear pit was open plan except for the skipper and first mates with cabins at the stern, one each side. The rest of the ten crew picked as best we could from the twelve remaining bunks, six starboard, six port on two levels with the engine, food storage, fridges and galley down the centre.

The bunks mid-ships get less bouncing and jarring when the yacht pitches over waves but they're next to the galley and can be noisy. The forward bunks are below the sail hatch, so if there's a sail change in bad weather you will definitely get wet, so the best option seemed to be the stern bunks just forward of the cabins and the upper port side was available. I couldn't understand why nobody had grabbed it until we set sail and my head was right under the main winch. There's a regular loud ratchet rattle as the crew tighten the sail and an even louder crack as the tension in the sheet (rope) is released to ease the sail but after a few days of four hours on, four off, I never heard a thing.

The following day all eight yachts were in and we were due to leave in three days time, which gave me time to get to know my fellow shipmates. We all had dinner together that night and it was obvious I was on the right yacht, what a bunch of piss heads – thanks Tom.

Jim asked if I knew any good bars and I pointed to the one a couple of doors away where Kim worked. All the lads were up for it as Kim was working and looking absolutely stunning. She served our drinks then sat next to me and held my hand and whispered goodbye and good luck.

"How long have you been here?" whispered Jim.

"Three days"

"Don't hang about do you, has she got a sister about my age?"

The last night in Tahiti was party night as we weren't due to start the race until midday. We all ambled back to the yachts about one in the morning, most went to bed and a few of us sat on deck under the stars chatting for ten minutes and finishing the last of the beers.

The yachts were moored 'stern to', in other words backed up to the dock with the anchor dropped to hold the bow steady. As we didn't have a gang plank the stern of the yacht was pulled close to the dock with only a squeaky fender for protection. The squeak was ten times louder inside the yacht so each night we let the yacht forward about 3 feet from the dock. Jim had counted the crew of 13 on board but must have been seeing double. There was a yell and a splash about 2am as a pissed-up Pete tried to jump the gap and missed.

I won't bore you with the details of all the crew; although each of them brought something to the adventure there were those that stood out more than others.

Most of the time on a racing yacht you live at about 20-30 degrees off the vertical to one side or the other depending which 'tack' we are on, so tacking can take the yacht through about 40-60 degrees.

The 'heads', or toilet and shower, were located at opposite sides of the hull, one port and one starboard. It worked best to use the one on the lower side of the boat, it was more comfortable, or perhaps less uncomfortable, as you could wedge yourself against the outer wall of the yacht.

The best time to take a shower was when you knew we were going to stay on the same tack for a while. Bill had worked this one out and decided he had time for a leisurely shower, his parting words before entering the head were "just keep this fucking boat steady for ten minutes, if you can".

Red rag to a bull; we weren't intending to tack but a few minutes later decide we would. We swung the boat over through 40 odd degrees, there was a loud crash as the door of the head flew off followed by a naked, soap covered mountain of a man spluttering some expletives that even I had never heard before, or as one rather posh lady crew member said 'covered in foam and foul language'.

And yes he did get his own back; covered our bunks with flour during the night watch so as you roll quietly into them you don't notice it but it sticks to a salty, sweaty body like shit to a blanket and you have to really scrub to get it off.

Everybody had a go at most jobs on board and on a calm day we let Carolyne have the wheel. Having her around was a bit like having the radio on, she never stopped talking and couldn't concentrate on steering as we zig-zagged across the Pacific and it's the helmsman's job to follow the correct course to the finishing line.

As the two crews changed watch we all ate dinner together and in an attempt to shut her up the skipper said "Carolyne, what course are we on?"

"Oh, I think it's pudding next darling!" came the answer.

We did have a serious word with one rather large lady who insisted on wearing a tiny bikini and who obviously didn't shave, not even a bikini line; it was like trying to cover a haystack with a postage stamp.

CHAPTER SIXTEEN

L eaving Tahiti and racing to Tonga would take about six days if the weather was with us, unfortunately it wasn't.

The first couple of days the weather was kind with a good breeze and big rolling seas. If the swell is with you the yacht will pick up from the stern and surf along the wave gaining a good few extra knots of speed. The challenge was on to see who would be first to break 15 knots.

As the newcomer I thought it would be only fair to volunteer for mother watch so I had 24 hours getting to know the boat and all of the crew on both watches. Plus the fact there's a better chance of fresh food ingredients for the first 2 or 3 days then it's frozen or dried.

Not being too sure what the meat was (probably goat) I decided on a casserole and was preparing the ingredients when, to my pleasant surprise, Jim said "there's a box of red wine in that locker, it helps add flavour to the grub, oh and we allow mother watch a glass each when cooking dinner". The surprise was that racing yachts are always 'dry boats' so no booze on board. Actually the wine was more like vinegar, but what the hell it was 13% vinegar!

The following day I fell into the watch routine of four hours on, four hours off during the night 20.00 to 08.00 and six hour watches during the day; so each watch moved on one and nobody was stuck with the same watch every day, particularly 'dog watch' midnight to 04.00.

In good weather three crew members were enough on watch which gave the others the chance to catch up on some much needed sleep. Although we had four hours off watch at night it took 30 minutes to get into the gear and 30 minutes to get out of it and the salt washed off so at best we only had three hours sleep between watches.

When I said 'six days if the weather was with us, unfortunately it wasn't' I wasn't joking

Exactly half way between Tahiti and Tonga we were caught in cyclone Leo. Having anticipated its' movements we steered a course to the north to try and avoid the worst of it. Unfortunately it reversed course and we were in it; 70mph winds and 40 foot seas. Everything was fastened down and we were sailing at 10 knots on a storm jib, which isn't much bigger than a tablecloth.

The storm hit us so quickly we still had the Genoa up (the triangular sail fixed at the bow of the yacht). As Mark and I were dropping and unhanking it the wind caught it and took it over the side except for the last two hanks which were still holding fast. It took six big lads all of their strength to pull a soggy sail back on board before we lost it. Worse still it could have gone under the yacht and wrapped around the rudder. Without steering we would definitely have capsized from just one of those waves hitting us broad side on.

The yacht was pitching so violently that as the bow of the yacht dived we lost contact with the deck and as it rose again we hit it with an almighty crash and as we went under the waves it was difficult to breathe, we were literally under water holding our breath.

There were just three of us on watch that night Mark, Johnny and yours truly, taking it in turns to steer every 30 minutes. As Johnny and me sat with our backs to the bulkhead to avoid the worst of the sea washing over us Mark looked up and said "Oh fuck!"

A massive wave came over the top of the yacht, almost as if we had sailed under a breaking 40 foot wave. As I was washed down the cockpit I passed Mark holding on to the wheel with his body almost horizontal as the water rushed past him. As I passed him I grabbed his legs and jammed my arse against the back rails (what a bruise I had).

The next thing we heard was the radio 'This is Sydney coastguard, Diana down, Diana down, any boats at the following coordinates please respond.'

There is an automated alarm system on ocean yachts called an EPIRB (emergency position indicating radio beacon) which when immersed in saltwater for a period of time goes off, and ours had.

There was a Vietnamese cargo ship about two days sail from us that offered to divert and 'pick up any survivors'. I can't tell you what a chill those words still sends down my spine.

By this time Jim was up and on the radio, "Sydney coastguard this is Diana, we're OK, a little soggy round the edges but afloat and sailing" If he thought this was a little soggy I'd hate his idea of soaking bloody wet!

"Diana this is Sydney coastguard, good to hear from you, we scrambled the choppers but they can't carry enough fuel to get to you and back, good luck"

"OK guys we're on our own, just keep her as steady as possible into the waves, forget the course."

About twelve hours later the storm suddenly stopped, the sea was calm and the sky dark grey.

"Tack, come about" yelled Jim. "We're through it, aren't we?"

"We're in the eye, it'll hit us again from the other side".

About fifteen minutes later it did and kept hitting us for another 24 hours.

There were some light hearted moments looking back, although not at the time. One guy, who had not done any foul weather sailing found it too much to handle, he was constantly sea sick and struggled to keep water down. He would occasionally eat a Mars bar because it was the only thing that tasted good coming back!!!

As we sailed away from the cyclone things got back to normal and I'd struck up a friendship with a real bubbly personality called Tara, small dark hair, not my style at all; she reminded me of Ellen McArthur, or maybe that was just because we were sailing. She'd been working in England in the catering industry for a year and was on her way home to New Zealand but decided to race a yacht there rather than take a 20 hour flight.

Tara and me were partnered together for mother watch, 24 hours of cooking and cleaning but no on deck working and a good nights sleep. We cooked breakfast together and cleaned the galley and heads, cooked lunch and all the time she was right there with me at meals sitting very close and as she passed me she ran her hand across my back or bum.

By mid afternoon everything was ship shape, the off watch crew were fast asleep we had time to chill out.

The skipper asked us if would check the sail locker and try get the sails we would need for the run to Tonga to the top of the pile. The sail locker is in the bow of the yacht which in bad weather is the most uncomfortable place to be as it gets all the pitching motion as the yacht rides the waves. Today was a fairly flat breezy day, which is why it was a good time to check the sails.

The forecast was good so we set up the large Genoa for a quick run to the finish. As I stood up and tuned round Tara looked into my eyes and said "Jase, you told me you had girl friend problems back home but this isn't home" and with that she put her arms around me and gave me such a sweet kiss. She had the most gorgeous bum which was nearly covered by a black bikini; and as the saying goes 'you can flog a dead horse but you can't beat a nice ass'.

I was only wearing swim shorts so it wasn't long before we were naked on the large Genoa, and boy after a whole week off did I have a large Genoa? She had very shapely, muscular legs topped with a beautiful furry brown bush, a slim waist and firm breasts with small, pink nipples just perfect for rolling your tongue around.

She insisted on going on top and I was so busy watching her breasts heave up and down I didn't notice half the crew staring down at us through the sail hatch, a big glass hatch right above us. I started laughing; Tara looked up, gave them the finger and carried on. She slowed the pace down and leaned forward to kiss me while gently raising and lowering her body over mine until I couldn't hold it any longer and we both hit the high notes together, the perfect mutual orgasm.

We lay there with my arms wrapped around her enjoying the gentle rocking of the yacht and the sound of the sea rushing past the hull.

The following day we crossed the finishing line and were first into Tonga, what a fantastic reception we got. This was officially the half way point around the world and the banquet that the Tonga yacht club laid on for us was spectacular. What wonderful people they really are.

It was good to get off the boat and have a soft bed and a shower that didn't throw you around. Tara and I shared a room to … er … save money.

The hotel was on a small island in the lagoon with cottages in the palm trees just back from the beach. Each simple cottage had a bed and a shower with a couple of wooden chairs outside on a small decking area with shade from the palms and a view across the lagoon to die for.

We could wade 50 metres into the lagoon and still be only in one metre of water with shoals of tiny silver fish around your legs.

The whole place was built from local trees with one large open-plan kitchen, dining, party room builts of telegraph pole size rafters with a palm thatch roof.

As I was sitting outside our cottage one morning two young boys about ten years old walked past collecting coconuts. One of them spoke English and offered me a coconut which I accepted and thanked him for.

Realizing that I had no means of opening the nut he produced from his belt a 2 feet long razor sharp machete and, holding the nut in one hand, hit it with the machete only a fraction from his fingers splitting it open but quickly cupping both halves so as not to lose the milk.

He explained that first you drink the milk, then there is a layer of 'cream' on the inside which you scoop out with your finger and eat, then throw the rest of the nut away for the pigs to eat. These small and friendly pigs were everywhere eating discarded coconuts and would even wander into the cottages, which had no doors.

CHAPTER SEVENTEEN

Four days later we started the second leg to Auckland which was quite uneventful compared to cyclone Leo. Tara asked if I would get off in Auckland and move in with her with a view to staying there and living together. The offer was really attractive, she was great fun and the sex was fantastic but we were living an adventure full of adrenaline not real life. I explained that I had signed up to sail to Sydney so that's what I would do but had no plans further than that.

We had a stopover in Auckland for four days which we spent together. I booked into a hotel just to get a comfortable bed and a break from the yacht. Tara checked in with her folks then checked in with me for four nights. I really liked Auckland and was tempted to stay but I'd signed up to go to Sydney so that's what I would do.

From Auckland to Sydney we hit the edge of another cyclone, Mona, not as bad as Leo but still pretty hairy, although having sailed through Leo nothing seemed scary any more.

As the weather calmed we had some fantastic sailing, particularly at night with the stars out and the swell from behind pushing us on. It's amazing how many stars are up there when you're in the middle of the ocean with no other light.

It was really quiet without Tara and strangely lonely. The rest of the crew were great company and a real bunch of piss-takers but it's not the same as having someone intimate with you.

"So what happens when you get to Sydney?" asked Jim as we cruised along at 12 knots on one of those balmy nights.

"Don't know" I replied "maybe I'll rent a car and drive north to find Rebecca. Maybe I'll fly back to Auckland and Tara. Maybe I'll fly home and pick up the pieces with Sam or Alex or Katie. Maybe I'll stay on board and sail further with you."

"You mean there's no girl waiting for you?"

"Nobody knows where I am except Tom and Ryan and they're under orders not to tell anyone."

"Tara knows."

"Yes and knowing Ryan as soon as any of the girls ask him nicely he'll crumple and spill the beans."

I knew I would have to make a decision, I couldn't sail around the world forever and never face reality again and maybe a new start on the other side of the world was something I hadn't considered until now.

The following morning the sun came up in a clear blue sky and on the horizon was Sydney Harbour Bridge. As we passed under the bridge I heard Jim on the radio.

"Sydney harbour this is Diana, Diana, over."

"Diana, good to hear from you, we thought we'd lost you out there a while ago, welcome to Australia".

Sydney was a ten day stop-over so the yachts could be lifted out of the water and have their bottoms scrubbed and the keels checked for damage. As we pulled into the marina there were crowds of people waving and cheering. All of the crew seemed to have someone meeting them here so I offered to secure the yacht while they got off and had a kiss and cuddle with their families and friends on dry land.

"Thanks Jase" said Jim "don't spend too much time tidying things, come and meet us in the bar just along the harbour, you can't miss it, it'll be the noisy one, we'll 'sit on the dick'.

As they wandered off I finished securing the yacht and tidying the cockpit when a beautiful voice said "Hello rep with the gorgeous legs, can we start again?"